LOVING LADY SARAH

As life returns to normal after the war, Lady Sarah Trenton's reality is put into perspective. Her love for Robert, the gamekeeper's son who has returned home safely, is as alive as ever. But they must meet in secret, for Lord Trenton, whose heart has been hardened by the loss of his son, intends to see his daughter marry a man of wealth and status — like the odious Sir Percy. The times are changing, but the class divide is as wide as ever. Will Sarah and Robert be forced apart?

J. DARLEY

LOVING
LADY SARAH

Complete and Unabridged

LINFORD
Leicester

First published in Great Britain in 2018

First Linford Edition
published 2020

A catalogue record for this book is available
from the British Library.

ISBN 978–1–4448–4457–3

Published by
Ulverscroft Limited
Anstey, Leicestershire

Set by Words & Graphics Ltd.
Anstey, Leicestershire
Printed and bound in Great Britain by
T. J. International Ltd., Padstow, Cornwall

This book is printed on acid-free paper

Wish You Were Here

Sarah looked around at the many seated figures in the old barn. Of course, she wasn't really expecting him to be there, even though both his parents and younger sister were.

'More tea, Joe?' she asked, holding the large enamel teapot over the empty mug at the old farm worker's elbow.

'Yes please, my lady Sarah,' he said, with that air of deference which seemed so misplaced nowadays. 'That corn dust gets right to the back of yer throat.'

The barn, with its vast arched timbered roof supported by immense, sturdy oak pillars was not, in its way, unlike a cathedral; a cathedral where people, like congregants, had come to celebrate and give thanks for the success of their labours.

Two long tables had been set out in the centre of the barn, and this was where people were now seated, enjoying

1

being waited on by the occupants of Merefield Hall, as was the tradition.

It had been a hit and miss sort of summer. After the promise of spring, when higher than average temperatures and days of unbroken sunshine had given further hope and expectation which the end of the war had already begun, 1946 — in this part of England at least — was reverting back to type, weather-wise, and it was a race against both time and the elements to get the harvest in.

Nowhere was this more keenly felt than on the Merefield estate where even Lord Trenton lent not only his support to his tenants' efforts but his hands, too, getting them as dirty as any of the men — and women — he now worked alongside.

But his reasons for this were not solely concerned with 'getting in the harvest', important as this was, but it gave him an escape from all the things tormenting and troubling him at present.

The loss of his only son, and therefore heir, in the last weeks of the war had been very difficult for both him and the viscountess, the Lady Patricia, to bear. But, whereas his wife, through her faith, was trying to come to terms with the situation, Lord Trenton had still yet to allow his heart to accept the tragic fact.

It had seemed so unfair, having come through over five years of war, to then fall, just short of the winning post.

His daughter, Sarah, had proved to be a rock to both her parents during this time but she felt the loss just as keenly. But her duties as a WAAF, working long, stressful hours at the nearby airfield, helped keep her emotions in check.

Besides, she'd had her own anxieties. There was someone else, very close to her, who had been putting himself in as much danger every day as her beloved brother had done.

But now, thankfully, the war was won and life could return, if not to normal, then at least to a more safe and predictable state of affairs — and the harvest supper would help to establish that familiar, satisfying and reassuring status quo.

If only there wasn't that other, newer, dark cloud closing in from the horizon. But today the family and all its dependants were not going to let this latest threat of 'invasion' spoil their enjoyment and pride in a job well done.

'I just wish he was here,' Sarah thought, sighing as she did so.

Separation and Secrecy

Later that afternoon, when the lunch was over and the barn cleared, Sarah decided to take her pony, Cymbeline, for a hack up to Westmoor wood, in the hope that Robert might be there, waiting for her.

The early September afternoon was still holding good. Once she'd scaled the steady incline where the wood stood like a green crown, she paused and turned Cymbeline's head to better take in the view. Despite the fact Sarah had lived here all her life, it still had the ability to surprise and thrill her.

'It's quite a view, isn't it?'

As Sarah looked towards the voice so did Cymbeline turn his head and prick his ears with a sort of knowing pleasure. And so now both saw the figure behind the voice as he stepped out of the shadows of the trees.

'Robert! I hoped you'd be here.'

Robert Penfold held out his arms as Sarah began to dismount, and she slipped gently down into his embrace.

'I've missed you, my darling,' he whispered, kissing her with a passion that separation and secrecy made all the more telling.

As they stood, holding hands, transfixed by a common bond of love, it was interesting to note the physical differences which concealed the spiritual similarities between them.

As Sarah was fair, so Robert was of an altogether darker complexion. Sarah's father had even said — whether unkindly or not — that Robert looked to have gypsy blood in his veins.

This was probably inherited from his mother's side, as his father, Lord Trenton's gamekeeper, was of a vivid ginger hue, the redness of his appearance also an indication of his temperament.

'How did it go?' Sarah asked.

'Pretty well, I should think. Obviously they're desperate for teachers and they seemed quite impressed by my qualifications.'

'Did you mention your DSO?'

Robert shook his head.

'No, it didn't seem relevant. And it doesn't impress everyone. Ask your father.'

Sarah frowned.

'Oh, that was different. And he would have been impressed if circumstances hadn't changed everything for him.'

'I know, I know. I'm sorry. Let's not go over it all again. I just wonder, that's all, when it will ever be right for him to know, about us, I mean.'

Sarah released her hands and distracted herself by apparently steadying the immoveable, patient Cymbeline. She was wondering if there would ever be a right moment. Especially now.

Robert moved closer, putting an arm around her shoulder.

'It'll be all right, you'll see.'

But such words were of little comfort to Sarah just now. Not with this other matter on everyone's minds.

'You heard about the compulsory order?'

'I did. I suppose it had to happen.'

'But why here?'

Robert looked at Sarah, who was still taking in the familiar and much loved view. It certainly was entrancing, with the manor house placed at its heart amidst parkland conceived by none other than the great Capability Brown.

'People will need houses wherever they are,' he explained. 'The war saw to that. And it won't be too close. Those orchards were past their best, anyway.'

'Daddy's never going to come to terms with it. He feels the whole fabric of society is collapsing.'

'My father's none too pleased, either — as you can imagine.' He pulled her gently towards him. 'It's the future, darling. It's what we fought for — progress, and a better world for our children.' He cupped her chin so that she looked up into his eyes. Despite herself, she smiled.

'That's my girl,' he said, smiling too.

And, for the moment, everything was good again.

Keeping Love Alive

The year 1947 started with little indication of what was to come. Everyone was used to the cold and made provision for it, stockpiling logs and keeping their home fires burning fairly constantly.

Work had begun on clearing one of the apple orchards, the workmen benefiting from the many bonfires the fallen trees provided.

Lord Trenton observed the proceedings on a daily basis, sometimes accompanied by his gamekeeper, Jack Penfold. They stood side by side in marked physical contrast to each other.

The death of his son had had a sort of wilting effect on Lord Trenton. His was actually a tall, slim physique whereas Penfold was shorter and stockier. He had the look of a pugilist about him and in his Navy days he'd been a boxer, winning trophies for his efforts — but now they looked to be the same height.

'It's a hard sight to bear, my lord,' the gamekeeper said sympathetically.

Lord Trenton said nothing for a moment, his gaze fixed ferociously on the destruction below.

'What's that son of yours up to these days?' he suddenly demanded, the unspoken implication being that Robert could not possibly be up to any good.

Penfold shifted uncomfortably.

'Some nonsense about being a teacher. A teacher!'

Lord Trenton turned to face his employee.

'He's the one who needs the learning, Penfold. He needs to learn to stay away from my daughter. D'you hear me?'

'I do, my lord.'

'Well make sure you pass it on.' He turned his attention back to the conflagration below. The rising flames, even from that distance, were reflected in the viscount's angry eyes.

★   ★   ★

'That's such a bitter wind,' Elizabeth Penfold said, as she hurriedly returned to the cottage having fed the chickens.

Robert, kneeling on the flagstone floor as he tied the laces of his boots, looked up at his mother, waiting. She often said things that had more meaning than was at first implied, and this was to be no exception.

'There's worse to come,' she added, giving her son a significant look. It was probably true that she had Romany blood running through her veins.

She'd met her husband when she was taken on at the estate as a scullery maid, but she'd never spoken much about her past. It was the future where her interests seemed to lie, and what she'd just said wasn't lost on Robert.

He stood up and, not meeting her eye, announced he was off to Westmoor wood where there'd been a sighting of a waxwing.

'Don't try to catch it,' his mother warned. 'Such beautiful creatures are best left free.'

Robert sighed.

'I have no intention of trying to catch it,' he said.

'Be careful is all I'm saying.' With that, she turned from him, and headed for the kitchen.

⋆ ⋆ ⋆

This harsh weather was making it difficult for Robert and Sarah to meet, especially as Lord Trenton had made it abundantly clear he wasn't welcome at the manor house. Equally, Sarah could hardly visit Robert in his own home. Even in 1947 it just wasn't done.

As frosts can wither and kill the less hardy, so too can love be in danger of dying especially when there is nowhere for the lovers to go.

Sarah couldn't even bring out her beloved Cymbeline in this treacherous weather, so it was to the woods she walked to meet Robert, her breath floating out ahead of her as she went.

He was, of course, already there and

ran to her as she entered the familiar pathway among the trees. As they embraced, the warmth of their breaths seemed to act as a catalyst in melting their hearts — hearts which were buried under layers of winter clothing.

'How are things?' Robert asked.

'Let's keep walking,' Sarah suggested. 'It's too cold to stand around.'

Arm in arm they made their way deeper into the wood. The wind was less able to penetrate this far in, which for Sarah at least brought a rosy glow to her cheeks.

'Daddy's very upset at seeing the orchard grubbed out.'

'I'm sure he is. My father keeps going on about it and somehow manages to blame me for it.'

Sarah stopped, turning to face Robert.

'I can see why,' she said, without thinking.

Robert was astonished.

'Really? Why?'

Sarah shook her head.

'Well, your views are so modern. Oh, I don't know, it just seems sometimes that everything's against us. Even the weather.' She shivered. 'And the subterfuge. I hate it, hate it.' Tears pricked her eyes. 'We're supposed to be in love and all I feel is despair.'

Robert pulled her towards him.

'It won't always be like this, my darling,' he assured her quietly. 'Your father's still grieving . . .'

'But it's so unfair,' Sarah said. 'Everyone seems to blame you for things you've had no hand in.'

'Even you, it would seem.'

She pulled away and stood with her back to him.

'I don't blame you, of course I don't. It's just, sometimes, it all seems so hopeless.'

Better Things to Come?

Mrs Penfold's prediction of there being 'worse to come' certainly proved true as far as the weather was concerned. By the last week in January the winter had the country firmly in its icy grip.

This made things even harder for Sarah and Robert. Ordinarily she would attend church in the village, giving her a brief opportunity of at least seeing and conversing — and arranging to meet — with Robert.

But the snow which had come, driven further by a biting easterly wind, had blocked the narrow arteries that connected property to property, making it impossible for all but the most urgent and necessary tasks to be attempted.

Robert, now a full-time student at the distant teacher-training college, found himself unable to come home for the weekends as he usually did. The winter weather was putting a hold on so many things people had formerly taken for granted.

Sarah, left to herself, found she was much taken up with domestic responsibilities which had formerly been her mother's domain but Lady Trenton now seemed less interested in dealing with those matters.

Finally spring arrived and with it, better weather. Sunshine, when it came, though not always warm, gave an indication — a hope — of better things to come.

Robert was sharing this optimistic mood as he travelled back from college, the prospect of a three week break presenting all sorts of possibilities to him, not least of which would be spending time — precious time — with Sarah.

She, too, was noticing the welcome changes in the weather as she, at long last, was able to take Cymbeline out on a hack.

Everywhere the signs were good. Birds sang and the hedgerows and smaller trees were each wearing a pale green veil as the new leaves unfurled.

In the woods the giants — the beech and the oak — hung fire with their canopied spread, allowing first the celandine, then the anemone, to bloom. It was altogether a good time to be alive.

Robert was greeted by his mother with all the warm affection that she felt so keenly for her son. His father, though, managed only a voiceless, cursory nod.

'Any news?' Robert asked, directing the question at his mother. The response, however, came from his father.

'Lady Sarah's more or less running things up at the Hall these days, on account of the viscountess not being as strong as she was.'

'That's a shame,' Robert said, genuinely concerned.

'What's a shame?'

Robert frowned.

'It's a shame that Lady Patricia isn't able to do things as she used to.'

'I expect you're hungry after your journey,' Mrs Penfold intervened, sensing the charged atmosphere between father and son.

'We're not ready to eat yet,' Jack snapped. 'I'm sure Robert wants to hear the rest of our news.'

'Of course I do,' Robert said, conscious of his mother's unease.

'You know they had to cancel the Hunt Ball due to the bad weather. Well, Lord Trenton has decided to go ahead with it this coming Saturday.'

There was a deliberate pause here, as Penfold watched for any signs of a reaction from his son. But Robert remained silent, not playing his father's game.

'He's decided — his lordship, that is — to make it a sort of benefit ball, with all money going towards the RAF benevolent fund.'

'That's both understandable and generous of him.'

'Oh, indeed it is. And there'll be some very special — important — people attending, not least Sir Percy Fywell-Bennet, you know, the baronet what lives over at Fywell Manor at Moldrake.'

'I don't know him, actually,' Robert

said, who, despite his best efforts, had flinched at his father's grammatical slip — something which did not go unnoticed by the gamekeeper.

'What's the matter, boy? Have I said something wrong?' He leaned forward towards his son in an aggressive manner.

'Don't start, Jack ... ' Elizabeth Penfold said, stepping in between the two seated figures. 'He's just come home. Let's have a bit of peace, can't we.'

Jack Penfold sprang from his chair.

'I know what he's thinking,' he yelled, wagging an accusing finger at his son. 'He thinks he's better than us. He thinks we're not good enough for him. Well, let me tell you something, my boy, you're the one not good enough — not good enough for Lady Sarah, so you'd better keep away from her or else there's going to be trouble!' With that, he stormed out of the cottage.

Mrs Penfold moved towards Robert and put both hands on his shoulders.

'Take no notice, dear, he doesn't mean nothing by it. It's been a hard winter and there's been a lot to do just to get things back as they were. He'll calm down soon enough, you'll see.

Robert stood up.

'It doesn't matter, Mum,' he said, smiling and trying to make light of it. But it did. Ever since he and Sarah had fallen in love he'd seemed to have fallen out with those he should still be on good terms with.

It was as if their relationship was cursed, that they'd become star-crossed lovers like Hero and Leander or Catherine Earnshaw and Heathcliff.

But no, he could not think along those lines. No, he would go back to Westmoor wood where, in a letter he'd sent to Sarah from college, he had suggested a time on this his returning day to meet. He would go now and wait for her, certain in the knowledge that love overcomes everything.

Suspicion

Robert was seated at the foot of one of the beech trees that stood on the fringes of Westmoor wood. From here he had a good view of the surrounding countryside, so that when Sarah did arrive, he would easily spot her.

Although she hadn't replied to his letter he felt that was due not to a lack of interest but because of all the extra responsibilities she had taken on.

In the meantime he sat back, enjoying the tranquillity of this favourite place. As he closed his eyes, his mind eased back to childhood days and the fond memories they evoked.

In a place as beautiful and timeless as this it was easy enough to recollect events, people and so on. He'd enjoyed a happy childhood, with the freedom to roam and explore the estate.

Back in those days, Lord Trenton was

a much more affable, accommodating man and he was happy for his daughter and Robert — the gamekeeper's son — to be friends and play together.

Perhaps his own experiences of World War I had made him adopt a more tolerant attitude towards the different social classes. Life was precious and there was much to enjoy — much to be thankful for.

As the years passed and games gave way to more serious pursuits, Sarah and Robert became conscious of their own changing feelings towards one another.

However, they both knew that, however liberal-minded Lord Trenton may have appeared to become, there could never be any hope of his condoning the relationship that his daughter and Robert were now embarking on. So a secret it had to be.

But with the passing years there had come a feeling of frustration at not being able to tell the world of their love. They tried to think of ways of making it acceptable to Sarah's parents but nothing offered any real substance.

And then came the war, and war changes everything. Meetings become moments, love fuels fear. The more you love someone, the more you fear losing them and the unbearable heartbreak it would bring. But they survived it and their love survived it, too.

If only Michael had made it, Robert thought, things might have been different.

A noise — a twig snapping — broke Robert's reverie and he looked about him to see what or who had caused it.

A girl was making her erratic way through the wood and as she approached the spot where Robert was sitting her expression changed dramatically.

'Robert!' she yelled, and ran headlong towards him.

Robert scrambled to his feet.

'Whoa, whoa, Sis, slow down for Pete's sake.' But she careered into him, her arms flinging themselves about him as Robert swung her round and round till their laughter and their lack of breath finally brought everything to a dizzy halt.

'When did you get back?' Helen gasped.

'This morning.' He laughed again. 'You silly goose, I've only been away a month.'

'Oh, I know, but ever since that beastly war when you were away so much and we all worried about you, I've never got used to you being away.'

'Come and sit in the sunshine with me and tell me all your news.'

He led his younger sibling back to the tree where he'd been sitting. He looked at her with that same pride and affection as a father might show, because in actual fact there was a good decade's difference in their ages which tended to make Robert feel more protective towards her than if she'd been nearer his own twenty-four years.

Her auburn hair — a mellower inheritance from her father — glistened in the sunlight. Come the summer there would be a spread of freckles across her face which would give her an even more endearing quality.

Oh, yes, one day she will break a few hearts, Robert thought, especially for anyone hypnotised by her crystal clear blue eyes. But all that was for the future. For now she was a regular tomboy who enjoyed everything about living in the countryside.

'Are you waiting for Sarah?'

'Oh, no,' he answered, a bit too casually to be convincing.

'Only she's gone over to Fywell Manor with her dear papa.' This last part was spoken with more than a hint of sarcasm in it.

'Fywell Manor?' Robert repeated. 'Isn't that the family home of that old reprobate Percy Bennet? What's she doing, going down there?'

'I couldn't say,' Helen answered, showing a genuine lack of concern over the matter. 'Do you mind? Only I know how it is with you and Sarah. And so do Mummy and Daddy, and of course Daddy's not best pleased.'

'You do talk nonsense,' Robert said, giving his sister a friendly poke in the ribs. But it was disturbing. He'd so hoped to see Sarah and had hoped, too, that she'd be as keen to see him, too. So what was going on?

*   *   *

Not even the bright spring sunshine, nor the healthier colour now showing on her mother's face, could lift Sarah's bleak mood. Her father's insistence that she should attend Lady Patricia on what he called this 'outing' had caused her to be suspicious of his ultimate intentions.

The fact that he was driving the Bentley himself and not using Dodds's services was also giving her concern. What is he up to, she wondered.

It was as if the bad weather which had caused Robert to remain at college at first for a week and then eventually a month had been the springboard for Lord Trenton to put into action some scheme, as yet unknown to Sarah.

Still, at least her mother was benefiting from the excursion. She had her window partially open and the fresh air seemed to be invigorating — bringing her back to life, Sarah suddenly thought.

For, although she seemed, through her faith, to have been coping with the loss of Michael, it had been evident by her physical appearance alone that it had taken its toll, in much the same way as her father's normally stiff and straight-backed demeanour had wilted.

Though, having said that, Sarah thought she detected a more positive approach to life in him just lately — a spring in his step, matching the season, a sharpening of the eye — all things which added to her misgivings.

They had been driving for some time along a narrow lane. Lady Patricia's arm was linked through Sarah's, whose hand, in her jacket pocket, felt for the letter — Robert's letter — which, in her agitation, she rubbed between her fingers as if it contained some mystical, magical qualities that could provide a solution to all her problems.

She longed to see him, yet at the same time, she wanted peace in her life. Her last spoken words to him had been harsh, but in some ways it needed saying — her feelings needed exorcising so that Robert might be aware of the dreadful conflict of interests in which Sarah found herself embroiled.

Like her father, she hated the idea of those apple orchards being ripped out and burned. Like Robert, her experiences of the war had made her understand and accept that times were changing and that there was a desperate need for houses.

There was an understanding that people of all classes had contributed to the defeat of Hitler, and that deference was becoming a thing of the past.

Unpleasant Prospect

The Bentley suddenly made a sharp turn to the right, tipping the two women in the back to one side. The mixed hedgerows, after a while, gave way to a wider expanse of what appeared to be a driveway with beech trees standing sentinel on either side.

Despite its apparent grandeur, there was an air of dereliction about it all. Lord Trenton was constantly having to change direction in order to avoid the many potholes that kept appearing.

A little further on, the trees ended, opening up a view which took in the distant hills of the county and, in the foreground, where the driveway turned around a grassy circle, a house came into view: Fywell Manor. Here there was further, clearer evidence of this family's decline.

Of Georgian origin, in its day it

would have been a house of some substance and elegance. Glimpses of such a grand past were still in evidence but other things — the blistering, peeling paintwork, the cracked portico — were a clue as to the straits of its present incumbent, Sir Percy Fywell-Bennet.

'Why have we come here, Daddy?' Sarah asked, genuinely puzzled.

'Just need to see the young fella,' Lord Trenton replied in an uncharacteristically jocular manner.

They were kept waiting for some time at the solid oak door, unaware that they had been observed and were still being observed by Sir Percy from an upper window.

The butler, whose appearance suggested he doubled as possibly a gardener or general handyman, led them into the drawing-room.

Sarah immediately noticed the drop in temperature. There was a chill that suggested no fire had been lit in here for a long time. Her suspicions were confirmed as she looked into the fireplace where a pile of logs, thick with dust, sat on the grate.

Looking further, she also noted that there were various shapes on the walls in a richer colour than the rest of the wallpaper, suggesting that paintings had once hung there but for some reason had been removed and not replaced.

She shuddered. It was a very depressing room and she very much wished they would soon be back out in the fresh bright air again.

Lord Trenton paced about the room, preoccupied, it would seem, judging by the taut expression on his face. Finally the drawing-room door opened and the butler announced the entry of their host.

'Ah, my dear Trenton,' he said, with that false bonhomie of the shallow man. His genteel shabbiness equally matched the room he was now in.

In his mid-fifties, thin, haggard almost, and with a mean glint in his eyes, Percy Fywell-Bennet had spent a single life in devotion to his own singular aspirations, which mainly consisted, in general terms, of all and any form of gambling.

Such a self-centred attitude had resulted in the near ruin of his estate. There were creditors losing patience with his excuses for not meeting their demands. But he was hoping that this would all be resolved in the not too distant future.

'My dear Lady Patricia, and the beautiful Sarah.' Before she could resist, he had taken her hand in his and pressed it to his lips. Both his lips and hand were cold to the touch, and she struggled to suppress another shudder which had nothing to do with the temperature of the room.

'You know we're having the Hunt Ball on Saturday week?' Lord Trenton said, who seemed to prefer to stand whilst he talked. 'We thought you might join us, didn't we, ladies?' It was a rhetorical question as was indicated by the way he now looked at both his wife and daughter.

'I would be delighted.' The baronet

smiled, looking pointedly at Sarah.

'That's settled then. Right, we must be going. Got to look round the farm, check everything's in order. I expect you're in the same boat after that awful winter.'

Sarah thought that Sir Percy's boat was probably the *Titanic*, judging by what she'd seen already.

Back outside, Sarah breathed deeply, taking in lungfuls of the unpolluted clean fresh air. It also struck her as a perfect day for a ride.

What Does the Future Hold?

Robert had long gone when Sarah finally arrived on Cymbeline. He'd remained as long as his sister allowed, hoping but no longer believing that Sarah would appear. Eventually his own need for food equalled Helen's and they set off back to the cottage together.

After lunch, Robert went to his room to catch up on some reading. Searching in his satchel, he came across the last letter Sarah had written to him, nearly a month ago. He read it again now but it still offered little comfort or clue as to what the future held for them both.

'I love you, Robert, of course I do, but I love my family, too, and don't want to do anything which might hurt them in any way.'

No, but it's all right to hurt me, he thought, and then immediately dismissed the idea as both unjust and unfair. Sarah was facing a dreadful dilemma and, in some ways, Robert felt he was responsible.

What was he thinking of — a boy from a working-class background whose father was an employee living in a tied cottage! It may no longer be 1847 but 1947 hadn't changed so much that their relationship could ever be considered acceptable. Yet what could he do?

He loved Sarah, loved her with all his heart. He couldn't just give her up on a matter of principle. He still very much believed in what the future had to offer — their future — but that only highlighted the problems and prejudices they were both facing.

Sarah's family history was one to be proud of, and recognised. She had a past she did not want to let go of, whereas Robert, having seen the horrors and destructions of war, could only focus on what the future might hold.

It was as if they were holding hands, as lovers do, but trying to pull each other in opposite directions. They were

going nowhere when he'd once hoped
that they were going forward together.

★ ★ ★

Sunday came, the weather held, but
Robert refused to go to church.

'What d'you mean, you're not going?
You've got to go!' Jack Penfold bellowed
when hearing of this. 'Is this more of
your so called modern ideas? Too proud
to kneel before the Almighty?'

Robert sighed. It was nothing of the
sort. He just did not want to catch sight
of Sarah when it seemed she no longer
wanted to see him. It was as simple as
that.

★ ★ ★

Sarah concealed her disappointment as
best she could, but the service on this
Easter Sunday seemed interminable,
despite its air of optimism and hope. All
she could think of was Robert.

After yesterday's ordeal at Fywell

Manor she longed to look into his handsome, open, warm features, to feel his strong arms around her, making her feel secure, to be kissed and kissed again, to hold his hand — both his hands — and tell him how much she loved and wanted him.

She felt the colour rise and flood into her cheeks as the realisation of what she'd thought dawned on her. Yes, she wanted him! Wanted him for herself, for ever.

Once the service was over she feigned a headache and persuaded her parents that she would rather walk back to the Hall than travel back with them in the Bentley.

'I hope you're not getting a chill,' her mother said, concerned. 'This weather can be so fickle.'

'I'm fine, Mummy, it's just a headache. A walk in the fresh air will cure it, I'm sure.'

'Just make sure you're back in time for luncheon,' Lord Trenton told her.

'I will,' she said, and then headed off

in the direction of the Penfolds' cottage.

She had no idea what she was going to say. What excuse she could possibly have for calling on them?

Then she told herself that they no longer lived under a feudal system. If Sarah wanted to call on a neighbour then where was the harm in it? But as she got nearer the property her nerve began to fail and she found herself at a halt in the lane, undecided whether to go on or turn back.

Just at that moment, the decision was made for her with the sudden arrival of Robert's sister Helen. The child had sneaked her roller skates in her bag and had managed to race along the empty lanes from the church. Fortunately, she saw Sarah just in time and so was able to avoid crashing into her. They both laughed.

'Helen! You made me jump.'

'Sorry, er, Miss Sarah, I almost didn't see you.' Despite the girl being in her Sunday best she still managed to look raffish — there was no other word for it, Sarah decided.

'Are you looking for Robert?' Helen asked in her usual direct manner.

Once again, Sarah felt the colour starting to flood her cheeks. This was ridiculous! She didn't know whether it was because she had been 'found out' or whether it was at hearing his sister speak his name.

'Oh, I . . . was just wondering why he wasn't in church this morning. Is he all right?'

'Right enough.' Helen grinned. 'He just didn't fancy going. And who can blame him on a day like this?'

Sarah, as daughter of the principle patron of the village church, could hardly condone the girl's comment, even if she secretly agreed with it.

'Oh well, as long as he's all right . . . '

'Shall I say you were asking after him, Miss Sarah?'

Sarah smiled.

'Just call me Sarah, Helen. Every-body else does.'

'My father doesn't. He thinks you're a princess.'

Instead of amusing Sarah, this idea of Penfold senior seeing her in such an elevated light was deeply troubling.

'I'm nothing of the sort,' she said a little harshly. 'Anyway, I expect I'll see Robert around so I can ask after him myself.' And with that she turned and walked back in the direction she'd come from. Her abruptness surprised Helen, who now wondered if she'd said something she shouldn't have done. She sighed.

'Grown ups! Who'd be one?' And she set off at a more sedate pace towards home.

Thoroughly Modern Mandy

The following week, much work and preparation was taking place for the forthcoming Hunt Ball. Sarah found herself caught up in the activity which, happily, provided a welcome distraction from other matters troubling her.

Robert had gone back to college without seeing her, and she could not understand why. Yet all the time she carried this burden of longing for him that was an ache in her heart.

On the Tuesday a letter came for Sarah. Her heart missed a beat but when the envelope was handed to her she could see it was not written in Robert's scrawly hand.

When she opened it, however, she was pleasantly surprised to discover it was from her old WAAF friend Amanda Miller.

She had written to say how much she missed Sarah's companionship and that, as she was on her way to Lavington in the next couple of days, it would be wonderful to see her again and have a good old catch up. It would indeed, Sarah thought.

It was Amanda who had taken Sarah under her wing when she'd first joined up, Amanda who'd given her an insight to the real world, to meeting and making friends with people from all walks of life. Though they all might have regarded her as a bit of a Grande Dame, with Amanda's help and guidance, she learned how to become part of a team, to be accepted.

Sarah wrote back straight away, inviting her to stay for as long as she wanted. It would be good, again, to have a companion of her own age and sex with whom, hopefully, she could confide.

★ ★ ★

Amanda arrived on the Thursday. Sarah waited on the platform at the local railway station to meet her, experiencing an almost childlike thrill of excited anticipation.

'Sarah!'

Like some sort of nymph arising, Sarah's friend's form gradually materialised from the steam evaporating as she stepped towards her.

'Mandy!'

They stood entwined together on the emptying platform, mutually delighted at the sight of one another.

'Cor, look at you,' Mandy said, stepping back whilst still holding on to Sarah, and giving her a scrutinising appraisal.

'Look at yourself.' Sarah grinned. They both laughed.

'Oh, it's lovely to see you, Sarah. I've been so looking forward to this.'

'Me too.'

Having left Amanda's suitcase at the left luggage office for Dodds to pick up later, the two young women set off up the lane towards Merefield Hall, arm in arm. The glorious spring weather still held good, and the birdsong all around them seemed like a fanfare of welcome.

Though physically very similar — same hair colour, medium height and of slim build, that they might have been

43

taken for sisters from a distance — they were worlds apart socially.

Amanda, or Mandy as all her friends and family called her, came from south London, growing up in an overcrowded terrace house with her numerous brothers and sisters.

The street and surrounding area was a close knit community which was why Mandy was so gregarious. Life was lived there and few were spared its beauty or ugliness. Nothing was sugar-soaped; you soon learned to face up to, accept and deal with all that came your way.

And then the war came her way, which brought those people, formerly worlds apart, into close contact with one another. And for some reason — in Mandy and Sarah's case — it worked.

They were approaching the open gated entrance to the drive which led to the Hall. Amanda stopped to take it all in.

'You actually live here?' she said, astonished. 'It's bloomin' lovely.'

Sarah almost became bashful. Though not ashamed, she was conscious that her life was markedly different — some, many would say better — than most people's.

Mandy looked closely at her friend, a small frown starting to crease her brow.

'Is everything all right, Sarah? You seem a bit . . . I don't know, anxious.'

Sarah struggled to keep her composure under her friend's scrutiny.

'I'm fine, just a bit tired. Things have been a bit hectic round here lately, what with the farm, and my mother . . . '

Mandy had laid a hand on her friend's arm.

'I understand,' she said. 'You can tell me all about it later.'

And, on this understanding, they continued on their way into the estate.

* * *

Lord Trenton seemed like a man possessed, a man with a mission. In some ways it was good to see him so enthused about things. It was as if he was gradually putting the past behind him and 'getting on with the job in hand', as he was frequently heard to say on his various sojourns in and around the estate.

There was a quickness of step that had not been seen in him for some considerable time. The death of his only son, Michael, had crushed him, almost literally, but now there were signs that, like the leaves on the trees, he was starting to open up again.

The damage caused by the severe winter weather had not been as bad as had been first feared, and the continuing warmth of the sun, and the lengthening days, was already showing results in the pastures and sown fields.

Lord Trenton's principle concern, however, was not with matters agricultural but was all to do with the upcoming Hunt Ball. There was still a lot to be done and, although things usually ran smoothly regarding any events at Merefield Hall, the Hunt Ball would call on more resources than Lord Trenton currently had at his disposal.

Sarah had been a rock in these

matters, organising caterers, managing all the finer details of decoration in and around the ballroom. It had also fallen on her to hire musicians, and here she found herself at odds with her father and the older generation in particular.

'Let's liven things up, why don't we, Daddy? People want cheering up after the awful winter.'

Her father appeared, at first, intransigent.

'This is not Ally Pally, Sarah. There will be the county's finest attending, and the last thing they'll want to be doing is a lot of jitterbugging.'

'But they won't be dancing much, they never do. And there'll be so many young people here who will want something a bit more up to date if they're going to get on the dance floor.'

In the end a compromise was reached. The usual stringed octet would be booked but Lord Trenton would allow some 'lighter' music later in the evening. But anyone Sarah chose would have to be vetted by her father.

'We don't want anything too loud or modern,' he insisted, which didn't give a great deal of scope for what Sarah had in mind.

However, now that Mandy had arrived — thoroughly modern Mandy — Sarah felt there was a greater chance of getting her own way. Mandy's forthright approach to both life and people had charmed Lord Trenton.

'Call a spade a spade, do you?' he'd said, with a rare and genuine smile on his face.

'If the cap fits,' Mandy countered with a grin.

The lightness of atmosphere brought about by Mandy's arrival had helped to lift a weight off Sarah's own shoulders. Now she felt equal to any task she had to undertake.

The only thing weighing on her now was hidden in her heart, and she wasn't sure if she could share that burden, even with her close friend.

Shock Sighting

It was the Friday before the evening of the Hunt Ball and there was little that could be done till the morning.

'What's to do round here?' Mandy asked, as she and Sarah sat in the two spoon-back chairs which were placed at the window of Sarah's bedroom, giving a broad view of the estate and surrounding countryside.

Before Sarah could answer, Mandy pointed a finger towards the horizon.

'Is that a fire?' she said.

A tall thin plume of smoke was rising up from near the horizon, dispersing at its top.

'That's where they're building the new houses,' Sarah said. 'That'll be the last of the apples trees being burned.'

'Is that your father's land?'

'Well, it was until the government compulsorily purchased it.'

Mandy shrugged.

'Oh well, people have got to live somewhere, and what better than somewhere nice?'

Sarah said nothing. She'd heard this argument before, from Robert, and she had no answer for it. They were right, they were both right. Why should a privileged few own all the best bits of England? But that's how it had always been, and it seemed to work. Robert's father was happy where he was — he didn't want to live in a castle and suffer all the consequences and responsibilities that such ownership incurred.

Keep telling yourself that and eventually you'll believe it, another voice in Sarah's head was saying. Why shouldn't people have decent, sanitised housing? This was the 20th century, for heaven's sake!

But, as always, Sarah felt such radical beliefs were a betrayal to her father and all he stood for. Nothing was straightforward any more.

The end of the war had, in fact,

brought more conflict into Sarah's life rather than the peace which she had, like everyone else, been longing for.

'Anyway,' Mandy said, reminding her friend, 'what's to do hereabouts?'

'Nothing much, I'm afraid. I hope you're not getting bored.'

'Not bored, no. Restless, you might say. You're making me too comfortable, Sarah.' She smiled as she said this, to show she wasn't serious.

'Where's the nearest town? I seem to recall the train stopping at what looked like a pretty busy station down the line.'

Sarah thought for a moment.

'That'll be Westover. That's a good twenty miles from here.'

Mandy raised her eyes to the ceiling.

'Ooh, the other side of the world then.' She sat up then leaned forward towards her friend. 'Why don't we check the train times and go into West . . . West . . . '

'Westover,' Sarah said. 'But we've left it too late. There's probably not another train till five o'clock.' The mention of the place where Robert was doing his teacher training was making her feel agitated.

Mandy stood up and stretched.

'Sounds good to me. I feel my dancing legs need some practice before tomorrow and I expect there'll be somewhere in Westover that'll just fit the bill.'

★　★　★

There was indeed somewhere in Westover that would 'just fit the bill'. It was a place called the GI Club, off the main high street and down a flight of steps. Even though there were no longer any American servicemen left in the town the club retained its name and identity, believing it gave a modern feel to the place which would still appeal to the younger elements of the area. And to judge by the present influx, it was obviously working.

Sarah followed Mandy nervously down the steps to the entrance door where a man in a lounge suit was stationed.

Above the cacophony of people's voices she could make out some sort of music, modern, and in the be-bop style. Mandy, ahead, was already signing herself and Sarah in.

Its status as a club was as fluid as the alcohol it served. Guests became guest members for the night. There was no actual club as such, which suited just about everyone.

Inside, the lighting was so limited that only the bar and small stage stood out.

'I'll get us some drinks, Sarah, while you grab a table.' Mandy then ploughed her way through, lost to Sarah's view as if she'd been submerged in mud.

Sarah looked around for a table and, as her eyes slowly adjusted to the dimness, made out what seemed to be a very familiar looking man sitting with a totally unfamiliar woman. She felt as if she was going to faint but managed to press herself against the wall for support.

The music was so loud and insistent in her head, the chattering, yelling, laughing voices were driving out all reason from her mind. She was about to make her escape when Mandy reappeared with a couple of Martinis.

'Are you all right, Sarah? You look as if you've seen a ghost.'

Sarah couldn't speak, so shook her head.

'What does that mean?' Mandy persisted. 'You are all right? You aren't?' She gave Sarah her drink. 'Here, knock that down you, you'll soon feel better.'

Sarah did as she was told and, in fact, the Martini did seem to have a sort of calming effect on her. Her shallow breathing began to slow and return to normal.

She felt she could dare to look again where the two figures who she'd seen had been sitting, but now the table was occupied by an altogether different group of people.

'Shall we dance?' Mandy suggested. But just at that moment the music ended. More lights came on, exposing the tatty seediness of the place. The bar had suddenly become very busy and the barmaid and barman, with their backs to her, were struggling to mix the cocktails for the thirsty mob.

'I've got a bit of a headache,' Sarah said, lamely. 'I think I might go home.'

'Oh no, please don't. The night's only just begun.'

'I'm sorry. I'll get the train back and then I'll send Dodds for you at eleven. How does that sound?'

Mandy thought for a moment.

'I can see you're not enjoying yourself, Sarah. But — I know it sounds selfish — I would like to stay a little longer.'

'That's settled then,' Sarah said, forcing a smile. 'I'll see you back at the Hall before midnight. Have fun,' she added, giving her friend a quick hug before she left.

★　★　★

It was gone midnight when Sarah's bedroom door was opened with a gentle creak, and Mandy's silhouette came tip-toeing across the carpeted floor. Although in bed, Sarah had not slept at all since returning home. She kept going over in her mind what she had seen — thought she had seen — back at the GI Club.

It was something that, even in her wildest imaginings, she could not have foreseen. But, then again, why not? What right had she to complain or judge?

She'd heard the Bentley gently crunching along the gravelled drive, watched as the headlamps, like searchlights, had beamed around the ceiling as the car rounded the grass circle before coming to a halt outside the main entrance. There was the sound of the door opening (Dodds always carried his own set of keys), a muffled goodnight and then a silence only broken now by Mandy's whispered words.

'Are you awake, Sarah?'

Sarah turned to face her but left the light off. She didn't want Mandy to realise that she might have been crying.

'How's your head, lovey?' Mandy asked.

'It's improving. How did you get on?

Did you have fun?'

Mandy sat on the edge of Sarah's bed.

'I should say. And I met this most handsomest of men. And the strange thing is he lives right here in the village. Robert's his name — Robert Penfield . . . '

'Penfold.'

'What?'

'His name's Robert Penfold,' Sarah said, sighing deeply as she did.

Even in the darkness Mandy could sense there was something wrong.

'You never told me what it is that's troubling you. Is it anything to do with Robert Penfold?'

Sarah sat up and Mandy took her in her arms as the tears began to flow.

'There there, lovey. That's right, let it all go.'

'I don't know what to do, Mandy,' she gulped between sobs. 'I just don't know what to do.'

'We'll sort it out,' Mandy soothed, stroking her friend's head. 'You see if we don't.'

A Vexing Problem

The morning of the Hunt Ball arrived and much activity was taking place. Various pantechnicons came and went, causing much disruption in the narrow lanes.

Robert was watching from his usual vantage point by Westmoor wood, and was vaguely amused by what he could see. One of them, unmistakable by its livery and colour, caught his eye.

Nothing but the best, he thought, watching the Fortnum's vehicle arrive at the front of the Hall — the front, not the tradesmen's entrance as the others were having to do.

He turned away and wandered somewhat aimlessly through the wood. He was feeling more and more of an outcast in the place he'd been born and bred in. He no longer knew where his relationship with Sarah was going — if it was going anywhere at all.

He'd not seen or heard from her for a week or more, and only knew what the girl Mandy had told him when he'd been chatting to her in the GI club where he had a part time job serving drinks.

It was hard work and not well paid. You got a break but there was no staff room to go to, so you had to make do with whatever seating you could find in the actual club.

Fridays were always the busiest nights. That was when they took on extra staff to help deal with the increased numbers pouring in. Still, it was something to do in the evenings other than more studying, and any money was better than none. It also helped take his mind off his personal problems which he was thankful for. The trouble was it was always waiting for him when he came back home.

Home. Again it came to mind how much where he and his family lived was conditional on their being compliant with the way Lord Trenton expected them to behave.

He pitied and understood his father's disapproval of his and Sarah's relationship. It must be a worry to him that, if he continued seeing Sarah, the viscount could use his overriding authority and have them all removed, leaving them homeless and, for Jack Penfold, without a reference.

Lost in these worries, Robert missed all that was going on — growing on — at his feet. Celandine shone with a glassy glow where the sunlight caught it, wood anemone were unfurling their petals, and stitchwort showed here and there, scattered like small stars on the woodland floor.

And above, there was all the feverish activity of pairing birds. Crows circled, arguing amongst themselves over who was the rightful owner of the reclaimed nests. Blackbirds and robins sang at each other in a war of warbles, each marking out their territory.

Robert, however, was, lost in his own

concerns, wondering where his place was in this world.

*   *   *

Lord Trenton was enjoying supervising the arrangements for tonight's event. A lot of it was actually being taken care of by some of his more experienced — in these matters — subordinates, but he still felt his was the key role in ensuring the forthcoming ball would be an undoubted success.

He had high hopes of bringing both an end and a beginning regarding his daughter's situation. The sooner she saw sense and finished with the Penfold boy the better. But if she wouldn't do anything about it, he certainly would.

Now that there was no son to inherit the estate it was imperative that his daughter made a good match, and Lord Trenton had already made preparations regarding that.

In the same way that he considered himself a logistical expert in organising

61

the Hunt Ball, he also believed it was in him to sort out his daughter's future, whether she liked it or not.

★ ★ ★

Sarah and Mandy were keeping well out of the way of everything that was going on downstairs. Until the flowers arrived, Sarah felt she was under no obligation to be involved, so she and her friend were now going through Sarah's extensive wardrobe.

'So many clothes,' Mandy noted, as she looked through just one of Sarah's wardrobes. 'How do you ever get to wear them all?'

Sarah flushed slightly, but without her friend seeing. It was a forceful reminder of just how fortunate she was in being able to have so much when, even now, people were struggling to live. But, despite her social position, Sarah was, herself, struggling to live — struggling to live within the turmoil of her emotions.

At least now she had someone to

share it with. After she'd cried into Mandy's arms the previous night, she'd shared with her the cause of her sadness and, although Mandy could not offer any practical solution other than 'I wouldn't let him go, I know that much,' it had been a comfort to her to know that she wasn't alone in all this.

It was also reassuring, in a bizarre sort of way, to hear that Robert worked at the GI club and wasn't in fact a patron.

'Have you seen anything you like?'

Being of very similar height, shape and weight, Mandy was able to take her pick of the many dresses and other outfits belonging to Sarah.

'You'll have to help me here, Sarah. I wouldn't know what's right, not having been to too many 'unt balls.' She turned and gave a cheeky wink to her friend.

'Right, let's see what we've got.'

And together they spent the rest of the morning trying various costumes on.

★ ★ ★

At Fywell Manor the morning was not going quite so smoothly for its resident incumbent. A screwed up ball of paper on the drawing-room floor was evidence of that morning's post having been delivered. Sir Percy stood in the centre of the room, biting his nails in an attempt to quell his mixed feelings of both rage and fear.

Before the paper had been consigned to the floor, Sir Percy had had the unpleasant experience of reading its contents. It was like many similar forms of correspondence that he received these days, except that this one — from his club — carried more of a threat of exposure and humiliation. Things were beginning to close in on him and he was becoming increasingly desperate for a solution.

There was, of course, the Trenton girl, and the old fool of a viscount was obviously keen to make a match out of them both. But it was a darned inconvenience as far as the baronet was concerned, a high price to pay (not that he'd actually be paying a penny should it come off) for his independence, to have some dratted woman busybodying in his life.

He was a confirmed bachelor but, in actual fact, there wasn't a woman in England who would want him, even without his debts.

He was so cold, so unutterably selfish that there was no-one whom he could call a friend. But that suited him. His only true friends were the cards and the horses, although neither of these were reciprocating his affection.

So, now he would have to do something about it. Or Lord Trenton would.

Out of the Blue

The Hunt Ball was proving to be a great success. All the best names were there. The county's hierarchy had all attended, much to Lord Trenton's immense satisfaction.

Even Sarah and Mandy were enjoying themselves. Sarah loved the whole tradition of the event, and in such an opulent and appropriate setting, too. She could not imagine, at this moment, there being any other way of life, even though a different sort of world was encroaching on it.

The new estate was going up apace now. She hadn't been to see for herself but learned from her father's observations. There was to be a school, a church, even a parade of shops. It was a good thing really, but it was not what she imagined so near to her own home. But at least tonight she could absorb herself into the fabric of this ancient, ancestral home.

Mandy, too, was having 'a smashing time', despite her total lack of experience in this high society. She managed to get by in one or two of the conventional dances early on, but she was saving herself for when the band came on later with some more up to date offerings.

Sir Percy Fywell-Bennet, on the other hand, was not having 'a smashing time'. He was becoming increasingly frustrated and irritated by the lack of attention which Sarah was showing him.

She had deigned to give him one dance but made it perfectly obvious that it was accepted under duress and she made no secret of her repugnance as she hastened from him without even the formality of a curtsey when the music ended.

He took that, as it was intended, as a personal slight, and he wasn't going to let the evening pass without getting back at her.

An opportunity presented itself at around the midpoint of the evening.

Bored by the whole event and wanting a cigarette, he stepped out on to the terrace. The night was clear and starlit.

He lit his cigarette and then noticed the figure at the other end of the terrace. Even though she stood with her back to him, her shape and form were unmistakable. Sarah! This was too good an opportunity to miss.

Discarding the cigarette, he made his way towards her as silent as a cat focused on its prey. There was a leer already fixed on his face as, placing a skeletal hand on her shoulder, he spun her round to face him. In that instant his expression changed dramatically.

'What the . . . You're not Sarah!'

Mandy looked up at his angry face, an expression of annoyance on her own.

'No, I'm not! And I'll thank you to keep your hands to yourself.'

Sir Percy looked even more outraged at this.

'You can't speak to me like that. Do you know who I am?'

'No, I don't — and I don't much

care.' With that, she marched off back to the ballroom, her purposeful stride a little out of character with the costume she was wearing. In her wake stood the frozen figure of Sir Percy, seething with a rage that would demand revenge.

★　★　★

The next morning broke warm and sunny yet again. To both Lord Trenton's surprise and delight Fywell-Bennet had belatedly agreed to stay overnight. To the viscount it represented an endorsement of his plans and he intended to make the baronet's stay as comfortable and as pleasant as possible.

His one misgiving — the single cloud in a sky of otherwise clear blue — was his daughter. She seemed not to be involving herself in Sir Percy's welfare — was, in fact, nowhere to be seen this morning. Most irregular. He made a mental note to have words about her unfriendly behaviour.

After breakfast — a moveable feast,

literally, as some chose to take it in their rooms and others, depending on their alcohol intake the previous evening, were gradually drifting down in dribs and drabs.

The morning after any grand event tends to be an occasion for introspective sobriety, and the only exception to this was Fywell-Bennet who expressed himself in need of a good, rousing hike in and around his host's estate.

'Get to know the place better,' he told the viscount, who wasn't quite sure how to interpret the remark. But best to please the fella, he thought.

Robert was already out on a hike of his own this morning. He'd wanted to see for himself the progress being made on the new estate. He was astonished to see just how much had been achieved. Astonished too that there was, now, not a single reminder that this place had once been an orchard.

There was a starkness in the view. About this time of year there would have been blossom and a few sheep with their lambs. It was such a contrast. But Robert knew in his heart it was for the greater good.

Families would one day take up residence here, breathing new life into the area, and benefiting from modern facilities in the 20th century. It was the least that could be done for people who'd made so many sacrifices for their country.

This is where he and Sarah seemed at odds, with her looking back and him looking forward. He understood her concerns and was very much sympathetic to them but life must move on, and if it was not to be with Sarah then he must learn to go his own way.

He turned from the view, heading back via the bridle path to Westmoor wood. Suddenly, all his grand ideas and principles seem to evaporate as, looking up, he saw Sarah. She was on her beloved Cymbeline and looked every inch the lady. And he loved her. Oh, how he loved her.

Sarah had seen Robert but an uneasy shyness overtook her. She didn't know whether to wave or not. It was quite obvious that Robert had seen her because he was standing stock still in the centre of the bridle path. While she dithered about acknowledging him, he waved and started to move towards her.

Cymbeline pricked up his ears and gently whinnied at the sight of Robert approaching.

Sarah now raised her hand, encouraging her mount to 'walk on' as she did.

'A beautiful morning,' Robert said, stroking Cymbeline's head. He was looking more into the horse's eyes at this moment than Sarah's.

'It is. I love this time of year.'

'I know, I remember you do.'

'Will you help me down, please?'

Robert stepped round and held up his hands. In a moment they were in each other's arms. But even now, in this close proximity there was hesitation on both parts.

Her familiar perfume was having an almost intoxicating effect on Robert and his heart was beating rapidly. Likewise,

Sarah was experiencing a yearning, a mixture of poignancy and desire.

'I've missed you,' she whispered.

'I've missed you, too. Oh, Sarah, I love you so much.'

With Cymbeline unnecessarily secured to a tree, Sarah and Robert sat together on the ground nearby. Much was being said between them, many misunderstandings being explained. It was as if they were in their Eden and nothing seemed to matter any more, except their love for each other.

'I have to go,' Sarah said eventually. She stood up slowly. 'I'll have to put in an appearance, otherwise Daddy will start getting suspicious.'

Robert frowned. He was as yet unaware of the viscount's intentions regarding his daughter and Sir Percy Fywell-Bennet but he would very soon find out.

Despite his ignorance of that situation, he felt a sudden urgent need to fully commit himself to Sarah. He got down on one knee and took her hand in his.

'Sarah, will you marry me?'

A response came not from Sarah but, firstly, from Cymbeline, who gave out an anxious whinny, spinning around on his tether as he did. The next sound which followed, again was not Sarah's voice, but an altogether different and menacing one, though laced with a sickening sweetness.

'What a charming scene,' Fywell-Bennet announced. ' Who do we have here, Romeo and Juliet?'

Robert sprang to his feet, incensed.

'Who the devil are you?' he demanded. Sarah put a hand to his arm in an attempt to restrain him.

'Don't, Robert, let it go.'

'Sound advice, my dear. You certainly wouldn't want to cross me, young man.'

'Who is he?' Robert demanded. But before she could reply, Fywell-Bennet spoke again.

'So you're the Penfold boy, are you? The one who's been causing Lord Trenton so much bother.' He used the word 'bother' to emphasise how unimportant

Robert was. He was thoroughly enjoying the discomfort he was causing.

'What business is it of yours?'

Again, Sarah tried to pull Robert away from Sir Percy. She was fearful of the consequences.

'I'll tell you what business it is of mine, Penfold. I have received certain assurances from this good lady's father, and I don't intend letting a little nobody like you getting in the way of things.'

Robert made as if to swing a blow at Bennet which caused the baronet to quickly step back a pace or two. But he soon recovered his composure, aware of the control he had over them both.

'I wouldn't advise fisticuffs if I were you, Penfold. In fact, my advice to you is to clear off and not show your face hereabouts again, otherwise your family might find themselves looking for somewhere else to live.' The threat was very real and genuine, and it was enough to silence Robert.

'That's better,' Bennet went on, thoroughly enjoying the hold he had over them both. 'Now why don't you just be on your way, back to where you belong, in your little tied cottage.'

Robert turned to Sarah, but her eyes were looking down at the ground, as if she were too ashamed to face him. And in that moment he saw how hopeless — how ludicrous — their situation was.

What right had he to ever think he could stand on an equal footing with even such a rotter as Bennet? He was out of their league, not in the same class.

Sarah's silence was further proof that he was totally out of place in their world. She was probably embarrassed by him. And to think that only moments before he'd had the nerve to ask her for her hand in marriage. What had he been thinking of? What could he possibly offer a girl who had everything?

'Do you want me to wait while you get on Cymbeline?' he asked, dispirited and helpless in this situation. But, again, Fywell-Bennet, with a dismissive gesture, waved him away.

Every step Robert took as he walked from Westmoor wood — and Sarah — felt as heavy as his heart. And with each step he became painfully aware that there was no going back now. It was over.

A Change of Scene

Robert's mood was equalled by Sarah's own aching heart. As she mounted her horse she took one last — longing — look at Robert as he made his way from the wood, from her. His demeanour, his posture, was showing his feelings. His shoulders seem to have dropped and his head hung low.

Fywell-Bennet was viewing all this with a very keen amusement. It was so enjoyable to see the pair 'so undone' as he put it to himself. And now he had Sarah in his power, she would have to comply with his wishes or suffer the consequences.

He almost laughed out loud at his good fortune. Things were starting to turn favourably for him. His luck was changing. It was a good omen.

★　★　★

'The swine! The low-down, rotten swine!'

Sarah became alarmed at the anger she'd roused in her friend by telling her the accounts of this morning. In her bedroom she was concerned that Mandy's voice, and what she was saying, might be heard in the rest of the house.

'You mustn't say anything,' Sarah pleaded. 'Please promise me you won't say anything. It will only make matters worse.'

Mandy looked pityingly at her friend.

'No, Sarah,' she reluctantly agreed, 'I won't say anything but I know what I'd like to do to him.'

In one sense it was a comfort to Sarah to have such a passionate ally, but, as far as she was concerned, it was all to no purpose. Nothing, she realised now, could ever come of her and Robert's relationship. There would be no happy ending — it was doomed from the start. But the alternative brought no comfort either. She would rather go into a nunnery!

'You're not planning on leaving yet,

are you?' Sarah was suddenly aware of just how much she was in need of her friend's loyalty just now.

'Well . . . I should be going soon. I'm meant to be seeing my auntie Vi — you know, the artist in our family. She's got her own place in Norfolk and she's been on at me for ages to visit her.'

Sarah felt ashamed at her own selfishness.

'You must go, she'd love to see you, I'm sure.'

Mandy's eyes lit up as she suddenly had an idea.

'Why don't you come with me? It'd do you good to get away, help you put things in . . . er . . . whatsitsname.'

'Perspective?'

'Yes, that's the word — put things in perspective. And you'd just love it where she lives. It's quite near the coast and the broads and there's so much space it's frightening.'

'Frightening?' Sarah was puzzled.

'Well, yes, for a city girl like me. I couldn't believe there was that much space in the country. And the sky! It goes on for ever.'

'Yes, I've often heard it said that that's why artists like going there, something to do with the light.'

Mandy shuffled forward on her chair and took both Sarah's hands in hers.

'So, what do you say, Sarah? Please say yes.'

'I can't possibly. I can't leave my mother, you've seen how she is.'

'Yes, I have, and you underestimate her faith and her strength. You really need to do this, Sarah, to get away — to get away from that vile beast. And if you do, it might calm everything — and everyone down. Besides, I owe it to you after all you've done for me.'

'Done for you?' Sarah was surprised.

'Yes. You've taken me out of myself. Before I came down here I was getting over my own problem.'

'What was that?'

'I found out my boyfriend had been cheating on me.'

'Oh, I'm so sorry, Mandy.'

'Yeah, so was he.' She grinned. 'But I was hurt, no two ways about it. But it gave me the chance to please myself for once and I really had missed you and all the fun we used to have together.'

Sarah sighed.

'It hasn't been much fun for you here, I'm afraid.'

'Oh well, never mind. Perhaps it'll do us both good to get away.' Again she took on that lively, earnest expression, shaking Sarah's hand as she did. 'Please say you'll come. Please.'

★   ★   ★

Lord Trenton was finding himself growing tired and not a little irritated by Sir Percy Fywell-Bennet's continuing exploitation of his hospitality. All the other guests had long gone, yet Bennet seemed in no hurry to leave, availing himself of all that was on offer, free and gratis at the Hall.

Lord Trenton lost count of the whisky and sodas he was getting through, not to mention adding himself to the table at luncheon, throwing Cook's kitchen into disarray.

The viscount also found it jarring how, whatever subject might come up in conversation, Bennet had a habit of taking over from the speaker and making it all his own, with all manner of embellishment.

Still, as he kept reminding himself, the union between their families was what would be best for all concerned, even if, as yet, Sarah was unable to see it. After all, it would be his daughter who, in the main, would be the one having to listen to the confounded bore droning on, and not him.

But even as he thought this, a small but definite feeling of contrition breached the self made armour surrounding his heart.

He loved his daughter, loved her dearly but, in the viscount's world of privilege and hierarchy, love in itself was an irrelevance. Family, title, that was what mattered.

He felt a genuine fear that the whole structure and fabric upon which this nation had been built was in serious danger of being lost.

And that was why, for him, there could be no question of Sarah ever marrying — or even associating in anything other than a platonic, respectful sense — with his gamekeeper's son. He would be the laughing stock of both his club and the House of Lords. No, it could not be — would not be.

The news of his daughter's sudden decision to go to Norfolk with her friend Mandy came as a surprise to Lord Trenton. It was only after his wife, Lady Patricia, rose to a spirited defence on Sarah's behalf that he grudgingly allowed it.

'One week, my girl, that's all. There's much going on hereabouts and you're party to it.'

Sarah did not like the unspoken implications in her father's words but she was, however, relieved to be leaving behind — if only for a week — all the troubles and complexities that life was throwing at her.

⋆   ⋆   ⋆

Dodds drove the two young women to the station. There was a connecting train which would put them straight in line for their destination.

The morning had started a little overcast with the possibility of a light rain shower, but as their journey progressed they seemed to leave the clouds behind, and by the time they reached Norwich, the sun was shining.

A bus ride was their final mode of transport, and from their top-deck seats they watched as the urban spread gave way to fields and isolated dwellings, with the famous broads serpentining around the flattish landscape. There was certainly a lot of sky, and soon there was a lot of sea for them both to marvel at.

'Here, jump up!' Mandy suddenly said. 'This is our stop.'

It wasn't far to Mandy's aunt's

cottage but it was difficult terrain over sand dunes, made more awkward by the cases each one was having to carry. But the weather was so bracing. The salt air carried on it the tang of seaweed.

'It's not far now.'

They were both gasping a little but were also extremely happy. If this was an escape it was a most welcome one.

Sarah was already experiencing a sort of reckless irresponsibility which was bringing colour to her cheeks and a lightness to her heart. It didn't change anything, but the change of scene somehow made her believe that things could get better.

Mending Fences

Robert, still feeling frustrated and angry from the confrontation with Fywell-Bennet, was further disheartened on hearing the news — again from his little sister — that Sarah had gone with her friend to stay at a relative's cottage somewhere on the coast.

'I think it's Norfolk but don't quote me on it.'

Despite his ill temper he could not help but smile at Helen's turn of phrase. Who exactly did she imagine would be hanging on her every word enough to want to, possibly, publish them in one or more of the influential broadsheet papers.

'Where on earth do you find things out?'

Helen tapped her nose.

'I have my sources,' which actually made Robert laugh out loud.

'That's better,' she said.

'Better? What do you mean?'

They were sitting in the garden, on the small square of lawn, sunk back in deck chairs, facing the continuing sun. Jack Penfold was out checking his pens whilst their mother was sitting at the kitchen table with her playing cards.

'You've looked so miserable lately. I can't remember the last time I saw you smile.'

'Well, I'm smiling now, thanks to you.' Robert didn't really want his sister involved in his own personal problems. Besides, there wasn't anyone — young or old — who could put them right for him.

Better to accept the truth — he simply wasn't good enough for Sarah. Her silence at his departure was a sure indication of that. As much as she maintained she disliked Fywell-Bennet, they seemed to close ranks against Robert, forcing him out.

He sighed. The sooner he accepted the situation, the better it would be for everyone. But it was a bitter pill to swallow.

Later that day, in an attempt to build bridges with his father, Robert offered to help him repair some of the fences that divided the various arable fields on the estate.

Jack Penfold's initial response was not encouraging but Robert chose to ride out the sarcastic comments so that, albeit grudgingly, Jack accepted his son's offer.

It can be a lonely occupation, being a gamekeeper, and it was made more so when Robert, despite his rural upbringing — 'nature red in tooth and claw' — won a scholarship to the grammar school.

That seemed to signal a change in the father and son relationship — not that Robert could be in any way responsible for it. No, it was Jack Penfold who found it hard to come to terms with having a son more knowledgeable than he was.

They had become strangers, more so

as the years passed when Robert proved to be a model pupil, always achieving high marks in his exams. His father would never acknowledge his son's success.

'What's the point in Latin? This is England. No-one speaks Latin in England.'

Robert knew that his father would never recognise that his son was doing well at school but had learned to accept that and live with it, so that, in time, he took no notice of Jack Penfold's hostility towards him.

They set off together in the estate Land Rover, a battered old vehicle which didn't exactly offer the most comfortable ride. Behind him, Robert could feel the warm breath of the gamekeeper's spaniel, Dime, on his neck.

Robert turned to look at him but the dog's attention was focused on the road ahead, even more so than his master who was looking all about him as he drove.

It was hard to tell if Jack was appreciating the late spring sunshine and the way it was providing a sharp contrast of light and shadow on everything, or whether his eyes were on the lookout for poachers and the like. Robert didn't know, and wasn't about to ask, so they continued their journey in the same stifling silence that they had maintained from the start.

The more formal agricultural fields finally gave way to a vast area of moorland and it was here that Jack's responsibilities mostly lay.

Robert was astonished at just how big the Merefield estate was, which made it all the more surprising to him why the viscount had kicked up such a fuss over the compulsory takeover of a few orchards. But that's how it is, he thought — the more you have, the more you still want.

'There's a gap here that needs sorting,' Jack said, pulling up rather abruptly. That was typical of the man, straight to the point but that suited Robert at the moment because, despite his best intentions, he didn't know what to say.

Robert got out and joined his father at the back of the vehicle as he hunted around for the tools and equipment he required to fill the breach.

Dime had leapt straight out as soon as the door was opened and was now somewhere amongst the gorse and ferns, frantically seeking out a scent, his stump of a tail a blur of excitement.

'Here, I'll take the wire,' Robert offered. His father showed no sign of having heard his son's offer but he thrust the roll into Robert's arms and set off towards the gap in the fence.

They worked silently together. Being the only two human beings in this immense landscape, their lack of communication was all the more obvious.

In fact, had it not been for the constant singing of birds — particularly an insistent yet melodious lark — the quietness of this sometimes bleak, treeless landscape could have been oppressive.

But working together, in this word-less way, was bringing both men back in harmony. Robert knew enough about this kind of work to know what to do. He had helped his father in the past and was enjoying doing so again. Neither got in each other's way; both were competent in their tasks.

'That's done,' Jack Penfold finally said, having stood back to appraise their work. 'That's done' was the best anyone was ever going to get from Jack in the way of recognition of a job well done but Robert was happy enough with what he got.

They inspected and, where necessary, repaired one or two other gaps, continuing to work in near silence. Yet Robert detected a mellowing in the atmosphere. His father, having been ill at ease at the start of today's outing, seemed more relaxed. Perhaps they were mending fences in other ways, Robert thought.

Jack Penfold reached into the back of the Land Rover and retrieved an old battered Thermos flask. Sitting in the driver's seat, he unscrewed the cup and poured out a measure of tea and handed it to Robert.

'Where's your cup?' was all Robert

could say, so taken aback was he by the gesture.

'I'll drink it from the Thermos. It's never too hot anyway.'

It was as though they were sharing a sort of communion, an unspoken peace agreement solemnised in tepid tea. It was a start.

★　★　★

The sea air and pleasing company was doing Sarah good. Mandy's auntie, Veronica, was a charming if somewhat eccentric host. Her rambling, fairy-tale, single-storey dwelling contained many of her paintings plus an assortment of what she called 'my findings', a term that described every object she'd picked up on her beach combing expeditions.

What was especially pleasant for Sarah was that no questions were being asked of or about her. It just seemed to be accepted that any friend of Mandy's was a friend of Veronica's, too.

It released that pressure which Sarah

had been finding unbearable — as though her head would explode with it. The weather was playing its part as well, which all added to the healing process. However, she was aware that this was no cure for her troubles, but at least it was giving her a break.

A routine of sort was soon established. Most days, after a varied breakfast, Veronica would either be off out with her paints and easel to try and capture on canvas that often elusive, mesmerising light, whether by the nearer sea shore or by the further broads and levelling landscapes.

Sometimes Sarah and Mandy would accompany her. When they did, Sarah would insist on buying them all lunch in any inn or hostelry that served food. It was the only way she might be allowed to pay her way, as Veronica was insistent she didn't want a penny for their keep.

On these outings, the three women would chatter about everything under the sun. At other times a magazine or book might hold the young women's attention while Veronica totally immersed herself in her painting. Whether or not she made a living from her craft nobody really knew, and were far too polite to ask.

Some members of Mandy's family thought she must have inherited some money from somewhere, but it was a vague theory.

On the last evening they all went to the local public house, the Jolly Sailor, where there was a rousing singsong taking place — sea shanties of course, accompanied by a little old man on an ancient concertina.

Some of the songs even Sarah knew and she joined in with as much heart and gusto as the rest of the assembled singers.

By around nine Veronica had had her fill and headed back home. The two young women — an unexpected and very welcome attraction to the mainly male patrons of the pub — enjoyed the good-natured flattery and banter. One young man in particular, who'd had his eye on Sarah almost from the moment she'd walked in, now approached.

'You have a fine voice,' he told her.

Sarah grinned.

'Why thank you, kind sir.'

'I'd like very much to buy you a drink. May I?'

Too Close for Comfort

It was the Friday of the week that Sarah had gone to Norfolk. For Robert it had seemed a lot longer than the few days she'd been absent. Apart from helping his father with the fence repairs, he'd had little to occupy himself.

In theory the Easter break was intended for studying but his mind had been so preoccupied with things that, often, he would find he'd read a whole page of a textbook without taking in a single word.

Tonight, at least, there would be a distraction, in the form of an early shift at the GI club.

Despite the cottage he shared with his family looking as ancient as the Hall itself, this was in fact the result of it simply being designed to give that effect.

It had actually been built in the early

1920s and, although in many ways it provided little more than a basic shelter, Lord Trenton had had the foresight to have a telephone installed, mainly so he could call on the services of his gamekeeper as and when he so required.

But it wasn't the viscount who called this Friday morning, it was instead Ginette, the full time bar manager of the GI club.

'I know it's short notice, Rob, but would you be a sweetie and help us — me — out?'

'How can I refuse when you put it like that?' He smiled at her referring to him as Rob — nobody else did, not even Sarah. And yet it was as if, by using that shortened form of address, she was implying a shared intimacy between them, one that he was unaware of, until now.

'I'll see you around seven,' he said and hung up.

His smile remained even after putting the receiver down. The warmth of

Ginette's greeting was proving to be a comfort to him. Kind words from an attractive lady. Be careful, he told himself. Be very, very careful.

★   ★   ★

'Ugh, I can't drink this. What's in it?' Sarah was holding her head in her hands in an attempt to stop it spinning.

'Get it down you, it'll do you good.'

The aroma of strong black coffee became a stronger presence in Sarah's nostrils as Mandy pushed the mug closer towards her where she sat, eyes closed at the kitchen table.

'Now I'm going to open the curtains, so brace yourself.'

Sarah screwed up her eyes even more, in a vain attempt to prevent the light penetrating. Her head ached so much. She'd never experienced anything like this before.

'There, that's better,' Mandy said, in that same cheery manner which Sarah was finding rather exasperating. 'Now, come on, be a good girl and drink your coffee. I promise you you'll feel so much better.'

'Do you have any aspirin, by any chance?'

'Sure thing.'

Whilst Mandy went off in search of aspirin for her friend, Sarah tried to focus on the events of the previous evening that had brought her to this state.

She wasn't normally a drinker. Her main occasional tipple might be an amontillado sherry or a port and lemon. But last night she'd sampled something much more potent. It was fortunate that Mandy was looking out for her.

In the crowded pub they'd become separated, time enough for the young man Veronica was later to refer to as 'the local Lothario' to make his move.

Already a little tipsy, Sarah had accepted his offer of a drink, unaware that his interpretation of such an acceptance meant more than Sarah would have intended or agreed to. But she was taken up with the whole jolly atmosphere of the appropriately named pub.

It had reminded her of how they'd celebrated when Winston Churchill had announced the end of the war in Europe, although that had been clouded by the news of her brother's death.

Luckily for Sarah, her friend had come to her rescue and led her from the pub. But as soon as the chill night air hit her, she felt an overriding desire to lie down which made the journey back to the cottage somewhat long and laboured.

Now, as she gradually recalled those events she felt a deep shame at her behaviour. She was glad that she would be returning home this afternoon, enabling her to draw a line under it all. She was just sorry that her friend would not be accompanying her.

Mandy was staying on at her aunt's for another week or so before looking for work in one of the nearby towns or cities.

The thought of her friend working whilst she continued to live the life of a lady was a further reminder of the divisions that still existed, even between friends. In that regard, the lady in Sarah was not relishing the prospect of the journey she faced by various means of public transport, in order to get home.

Once Mandy had come back with aspirin and water, and stood over her whilst she took them, Sarah claimed a need for some air.

It was a mean deception but Sarah needed to be on her own in order to make a telephone call.

She'd had to walk some distance before finding a telephone kiosk, but the bracing air seemed to be improving her physical condition at least.

'Hello, is that you, Foster?' Foster was their butler. 'Would you ask Dodds if he wouldn't mind coming to collect me? I'm afraid I've missed my connection and I do need to get home tonight.'

Foster assured Sarah that her instructions would be carried out and she put down the receiver, relieved yet guilty. It was all too easy to rely on others when you knew they had no choice but to obey.

★   ★   ★

Robert, too, had awoken in a troubled frame of mind — not that he'd had too much to drink or anything of that nature. No, what he'd experienced was a situation too close for comfort.

He'd gone into town, arriving in plenty of time to begin his shift at the GI club and was greeted by an overly effusive Ginette who came running up to him, placing a kiss full on his lips.

'Oh, thank you so much, Rob, you've saved my life. Come through and have a drink yourself, sweetie, before you get started.'

'A cup of tea would be nice.'

Ginette shrieked with laughter.

'Oh, you're such a card! Very well, tea it is.'

The evening, being a Friday, was soon very busy which made the time fly by. The only other girl who worked in the place, Paula, seemed often to be looking in Robert's direction whenever he looked her way, although she could just as easily have interpreted it as him often looking at her.

She usually shared her break with him, saving a chair for him if he'd been held up, as he would do likewise. He knew very little about her except that she was an obvious attraction to the place.

She looked a little like Lauren Bacall, he thought, especially when she adopted a sultry, pouting expression in response to a customer's flattery.

But it was all an act. She had no interest in the sort of people who spent their time and money in a place like this. Robert realised she was a snob; he'd never really known one from his own, similar background, but there was no mistaking it. And when she learned that Robert had been a pilot officer in the RAF she did little to hide her feelings for him.

Ordinarily he would ignore any such

posturing but, for some reason, he felt he almost wanted to respond to Paula's attention, if only because he was feeling the loss of Sarah's affection.

But of course, it couldn't happen, not really. He liked Paula as a workmate, but that's as far as it would ever go, no matter how vulnerable he might be feeling. It was just that Paula seemed to be sensing his heartache and wanting to do something to make it better.

'Do you ever feel you'd like to get away from all this?' she'd asked, as they sat at the table she'd bagged for their short break.

Robert shrugged.

'I'm not here that often to notice. Why, do you?'

'I do. I often imagine a cottage somewhere, you know, roses round the door, that sort of corny thing. A little flower garden, and someone to keep me company.' As she said this she gave Robert such a pointed look that it was pretty apparent exactly who the 'company' was that she had in mind.

He shifted uncomfortably in his chair.

'Sounds idyllic, but not quite real.'

'Maybe, maybe not. It's good to have a dream, though, don't you think?'

'Someone once said that dreams are for people who sleep whilst life is for the living.'

'I know.' She reached across the table and covered his hand with hers. 'But I don't think I want to wake up just yet.'

And then she withdrew her hand and turned her gaze on to the people milling around. Nothing more was said, the matter was closed. But, in the warmth of her appeal, he had come close, too close.

Subject Closed

'I'm glad you're back. Sir Percy's been pining for you.'

Lord Trenton's attempt at light-heartedness didn't go down well with Sarah. She'd arrived home late the previous night and had gone to bed without seeing anyone.

Now, this morning, seated at her place in the dining-room, she should have been feeling pleased to be back at the Hall, and she was, until her father had then chosen, rashly, to make such a tasteless comment, reminding her of how much he wanted the two totally incompatible people to become one. It was as if a black cloud had, in a heartbeat, blocked out the sun.

She ignored his remark, paying much attention to spreading marmalade on her toast, asking instead after her mother, Lady Patricia.

'She's well, but she did miss you, my girl. As we all did, including, as I said, Sir Percy.'

Sarah leaped to her feet, trembling with rage.

'Will you stop going on about Sir Percy Fywell — blessed — Bennet! I don't know what you have in mind . . . '

'I have the future of this family in mind, Sarah, which you would do well to remember.' His expression and tone were grave. Sarah could not hold his glare, so ran from the room, tears already spilling as she went.

'Sarah!'

But she was gone, leaving the viscount to dwell upon his mistimed efforts to get things moving regarding his daughter and Fywell-Bennet.

Sarah had gone to her room and swiftly changed into her riding gear. Not only did she need to get out of the house but she wanted to put a great distance between herself and her father.

The only way that was possible at present was to take her beloved

Cymbeline out on a hack.

Really, her father had gone too far this time, she was thinking, as she flung her skirt and petticoat on to the floor of her bedroom, the thought not occurring to her, in her anger, that somebody else would have the task of picking the clothes up.

She'd already complied as best she was able in not seeing Robert again (she could not bring herself, even in her private thoughts, to say any more) and she was painfully aware of the hold Fywell-Bennet had over her in that regard, but it was adding insult to injury to expect her to happily fall in with his plans for her.

She ran down the staircase in a most unladylike manner which would have incurred the disapproval of her ancestors, a number of whom were represented in paintings on the walls leading down to the chequered hallway.

Even Foster wasn't quick enough to be on hand to open the main door, such was the speed of her departure.

One of the stable hands saddled Cymbeline and after a matter of minutes Sarah was off, trotting out of the cobbled courtyard, under the clock towered arch, and away, up almost instinctively towards Westmoor wood.

It being a Monday she knew Robert wouldn't be there but her heart could not help but direct her to the place where they had shared so many intimate moments; spoilt now, of course, by the brutish intervention of Fywell-Bennet and his threat to expose their relationship.

Once at the top she rested Cymbeline for a few minutes and took in the view once more. It was a lot to give up, she thought, as her eyes gazed upon the familiar and much loved panorama. But hadn't she already given up more than she'd ever wished to, in giving up Robert?

Would she never be free of this torment? She thought of her friend Mandy and wished she were here now, to help and comfort her, but then she realised that she was betraying a weakness in herself, that in fact she slightly envied Mandy her desire for independence, which she was seeking by working.

Since the war ended, Sarah had found herself back in her place at the Hall, almost as if nothing had changed, but she was in some respects a different person.

She'd seen what life — real life — was like beyond the boundaries of Merefield Hall. She had discovered the 20th century and, although not embracing all of its qualities, was nonetheless interested enough to want to be more than an onlooker.

'What I need is a job,' she said aloud. Only Cymbeline heard and it made no impression on him. But it had to be a way forward, something to focus on. With this aspiration in mind she turned her horse and headed back down to the Hall.

★   ★   ★

Sir Percy Fywell-Bennet was pacing up and down on his already well-worn carpet. He was growing as impatient as his creditors with the lack of progress with his plans. Sarah was continuing to avoid him as often as she could (nearly, but not quite as often as he was avoiding paying his bills) and the old fool of a viscount seemed to have little or no influence in that regard.

Matters were becoming critical. Time was very much against him, but to the outside world — and in particular, Lord Trenton — he tried to keep up the appearance of a man of means and consequence.

Because Lord Trenton didn't move in Fywell-Bennet's dubious circles, he was able to some extent to create the illusion of a man of property and substance. In fact, he was nothing of the sort, something which hadn't escaped the notice of Lord Trenton's wife, Lady Patricia.

'He's not what he seems,' she told her husband, expressing her disapproval when they'd recently been discussing matters relating to Sarah.

They had both been seated either side of the capacious but unlit fireplace in the drawing-room, their morning coffees cooling and untouched.

'What do you mean by that?' the viscount had demanded, though he knew all too well exactly what she meant.

'Do you honestly believe he's a good match for our daughter?' The colour was back in the viscountess's cheeks. She had been growing stronger of late, as Mandy had predicted.

Lady Patricia could see the injustice that was being inflicted on Sarah but she also understood her husband's concerns for the family name, especially now that Michael was not here to inherit eventually. She had been more easily able to bring her son to mind than Lord Trenton could. He would never speak of him, as if he had never existed.

Their separate grief had never been united so that they might have been some comfort to each other. But now Lady Patricia felt that her daughter, at least, must not be another sacrifice. She would be her champion.

'He's a darned sight better than Penfold's boy,' the viscount sneered.

'In what way?'

Lord Trenton was astonished by the spirit his wife was showing. Secretly he was glad to see that she was involving herself once more in the matters and welfare of the estate. But he also could detect a wilfulness in her which he was going to have great difficulty in breaking.

'He's just not good enough.'

'Well, he was good enough to fight for his country and all that it stood for. There was no great advantage to him for putting his life at risk.'

Lord Trenton waved a dismissive hand towards her.

'You're missing the point, my dear. As a man I admire him, he's a brave fella, no doubt about it. I believe he even got some sort of award for his pluck.'

'You know very well he did. Why did

you not acknowledge it before? Jack Penfold would have appreciated you mentioning it.'

Lord Trenton was getting rattled. He always did whenever he was in the wrong.

'You are getting away from the point, Pat. Sir Percy is a respectable man with an estate not dissimilar in size to this one . . .'

'But in a greatly dilapidated state.'

He ignored the interruption.

'Sarah could do far worse than marry him. And just think,' he added, with an attempt at cheerful indulgence towards his wife, 'she'd only be down the road, so to speak, so I imagine you'd both be to-ing and fro-ing on an almost daily basis.'

He stood up, the subject now closed as far as he was concerned.

'I'm off to see what my gamekeeper's up to. Soon be that time of year again.' And, without another word, he left both his wife and his coffee.

Brief Encounter

Even by the next day, the idea of getting a job still very much appealed to Sarah. The problem was she wasn't sure what type of work was best suited to her.

She needed Robert's advice on the matter and considered it a suitable excuse — or rather reason, she corrected herself — for making contact with him. There had been no sign of him since she'd returned from Norfolk. He hadn't even attended church the previous Sunday.

She had almost convinced herself that he'd learned of her very unladylike behaviour at the Jolly Sailor pub and was disgusted by it. It was ridiculous, she knew, but it just felt so strange not to be in his company any more — not to have him hold her in his arms and say that he loved her.

Probably he thought that her lack of

response — her hesitation — to his proposal meant that she, like her father, didn't think he was good enough for her, and that even an insidious creature like Fywell-Bennet was a better prospect than anything Robert could ever hope to offer. But he'd be wrong.

Her love for him was like the sun — it shone brightly in her heart, and even if it went down sometimes according to circumstances, such as these now, it would always rise again and could never be extinguished.

Impatient, and in need of action, she abandoned the idea of contacting Robert. Instead, she dug out her old bicycle and without explaining to anyone where or why she was going, set off for the railway station. From there she took a train into Shepham, the nearest sizeable town.

As she travelled in the first-class compartment she experienced a feeling of excited anticipation, tempered only by the realisation that her choice of fare was likely to keep her separate from the type of people she would no doubt be involved with.

It had been different in the war, of course. Everyone had been thrown together, united in a common cause, and she had relished the challenges and opportunities it had provided for her.

But as welcome as the end to hostilities was, it had left her frustrated that her newly acquired skills were considered of no further use. She'd had to return to what was literally the old way of life.

It hadn't seemed to matter too greatly all the while she believed — naively — that she and Robert might have a future together, something she would engage in, one day at a time.

Now, though, with Robert banished, the future offered a much more frightening prospect and, as she climbed the flight of steps leading up to the entrance to the Labour Exchange, her nerve almost failed.

Just as she was about to turn and head back home, the door opened and a young man held on to it as he stood back, inviting Sarah to enter.

An hour later she came out, registered for employment and with the prospect of a few vacancies for her to consider. One stood out because it was for a school secretary. The only problem was, the school in question was still being built and so the position would not be available until September.

The school in question was the new primary complex currently under construction on what used to be one of her father's orchards.

If she went for the job and got it, it would be extremely convenient. On the other hand, it would be like rubbing salt into the wounds of her father's objections. He would see it as a sort of betrayal.

She sighed and looked again at the other two positions that might be open to her. Filing clerk or a timekeeper, both of which were further out of town and required an early start.

That initial feeling of enthusiasm and

purpose was swiftly evaporating. Again she brought out the card with the school vacancy. She sighed. What was there to lose?

* * *

Later that same day, and unbeknown to Sarah, Robert was on the same train that she was now boarding, heading home. He'd got on at its commencement, at Westover, his briefcase stuffed full of notes and textbooks.

The lecturer for his course this week had been taken suddenly ill and, in the absence of an immediate replacement, students were offered the 'opportunity' for a little more study leave at home.

Robert wasn't too sure about this. When he was away from home, attending lectures, writing dissertations, he found that he did not think as much about Sarah — and all that went with her — as when he was back at home where there were so many things, and places, which were a constant reminder of what might have been.

Having thought all these things through, it came as a shock when he stepped off the train to see Sarah emerging from the steam and smoke and walking towards him. It was as if he were dreaming. Her eyes when they eventually met his, registered a similar sort of surprise and disbelief.

'Were you on the train?'

'Yes.' He explained the circumstances which had brought him back home so early in the week. Sarah's explanation, however, contained very little that was true.

'Mummy needed something in town. I was at a bit of a loose end so offered to go and get it for her.'

'Where's Dodds? I can't see the Bentley.'

'Oh, no, I came on my bike. Actually that's where I'm going, to collect my bike.'

They were both conscious of the stilted and formal way they were talking to one another. There was an awkwardness about them which would have seemed unimaginable a little while ago.

It was as if they were strangers, that they had never met before until this moment, and there seemed nothing either of them could do to change things.

It was as if a spell — a curse — had been cast which prevented them ever again showing their true feelings — a curse that only a kiss could break, and that didn't seem very likely now.

Because the covered-in bike rack was adjacent to the exit, Sarah and Robert continued walking together. Neither could think of anything more to add, so they made their way to the bike shed in silence.

This is how things end, Sarah was thinking, with a whimper not a bang, and without being aware, she sighed.

Robert took it as a sign that she was already bored by his company, that she found him depressing.

He decided that as soon as they reached the bike shed he'd nip smartly away, possibly heading up the hill opposite the station and along the bridle path so that Sarah would not have to pass him on the road at some point.

But events were about to take a different turn.

'Oh, no!' Sarah suddenly stopped, staring at her bike. 'I've got a puncture. How did that happen?'

Robert stopped, too, and could see that the rear wheel was indeed flat.

'Do you have a repair kit?'

'I'm not sure ... maybe, in the saddle bag.'

Robert went over and undid the straps to the saddle bag. Fortunately there was a puncture repair kit in it.

'Ah, yes there is. Good. Now I just need a bowl of water to locate the puncture.'

'Oh, please don't bother, Robert. I'll phone home and get Dodds or someone to come and get me.'

'That won't be necessary.' Robert took off his jacket and handed it to Sarah without even looking at her. 'Now, if you can just go and borrow a bowl of water from old Beggs, I'll make a start.'

He rummaged back in the saddlebag and found an old silver dessert spoon, obviously from the Hall.

It was ideal, and evidently intended for the job in hand. Whilst Sarah was away fetching a bowl of water, Robert, with the help of the spoon's handle, managed to prise the outer tyre from the wheel rim, in order to extract as much as he could of the inner tube.

A shadow passed over him.

'Here's the bowl.' Sarah passed it to his crouching figure and, for a split second, their fingers came into contact.

'Thank you,' Robert said, taking it from her.

Sarah leaned against the brick pillar of the bike shelter. At first she looked everywhere except at Robert, but after a short space of time, her gaze fell on his crouched figure, and there it remained.

'Ah, got it!' he cried triumphantly. 'Soon have it fixed, then you can be on your way.' He was looking at her as he said this, suddenly aware of the hidden significance of what he'd said. Sarah felt it. too. I don't want to be on my way, she was thinking, not without you.

They continued looking at each other as Robert slowly stood up.

'I'd take you in my arms but they're a bit grubby now.'

'I don't care.' Suddenly they were embracing, kissing, holding one another in an urgent ecstasy of pent-up desire.

Eventually they pulled apart, but were both lost in each other, unable to see or to care about anything else.

'Have you managed to fix it, sir?' The apologetic voice of old Beggs, the stationmaster, shook them out of their reverie and back to the matter in hand. They quickly disengaged themselves, hoping that he would not be indiscreet about what he must have seen.

'Just about. Well, I've located the puncture, just need to patch it now. Thanks for the bowl, by the way.'

Robert tipped the water away and handed it back to Beggs who, thanking them graciously — as if they'd been the ones doing him the favour — shuffled back to his office and timetables.

Sarah and Robert grinned at each other before turning back to the matter in hand.

Once it was repaired Sarah walked some of the way back along the lane with Robert. Again, nothing was said, but this time the silence was not oppressive, it carried an altogether different, lighter atmosphere, as if there was a shared understanding, a common bond reuniting them once more.

After a while Robert stopped.

'I think we'd better part here. I can take the footpath from now on.'

'Oh, dear. I expect you're right.'

They looked into each other's eyes for a while, aware of the close proximity of their bodies, aware, too, of the close proximity of possible spying eyes.

Once again an invisible barrier was starting to come between them, even if, at this moment, they may have seemed unaware of it. But caution was taking over from passion as Robert stepped away, and without looking back crossed the road towards the footpath which would take him on a meandering and lonely way home.

Old Beggs from the railway station hadn't been quite the soul of discretion that Sarah and Robert would have preferred. In the Railway Arms, later that evening, he painted a very colourful and complete picture from the little that he'd actually witnessed.

'They wuz all over each other, I'm telling you. Couldn't keep their 'ands to theirselves.'

The more interested and curious his audience became the more he felt emboldened to embellish the tableau.

'He told 'er they'd allus be together . . . no matter what.' This last phrase was delivered with all the dramatic effect of a Laurence Olivier, and it earned him another drink.

Jack Penfold, never the most sociable of creatures, had been catching snippets of this performance from his isolated seat in the private bar. He wasn't sure whether to take his rising anger out on Beggs or save it for his son. Still undecided, he downed his whisky and stormed out.

Emergency at the Hall

The last week of July brought an end to Robert's studies. He was now a fully qualified teacher which made his mother, at least, very proud.

Jack Penfold remained silent on the matter, as he also did over the business at the Railway Hotel. Better to wait and see, he'd decided. That old fool Beggs was always coming out with one tall story after another, and it wouldn't do to call his bluff over what he'd claimed to have seen and heard with regard to Sarah and Robert.

It would only serve to reignite people's curiosity and suspicions, which might, like a forest fire, spread to and reach the ears of his master Lord Trenton. Let it go, he decided, a sensible option in the circumstances.

Lord Trenton was very much involved in preparations for the first shoot of the season. He seemed constantly to be at Jack Penfold's shoulder, questioning him daily about the condition and number of the game birds, and then coming along to see for himself, making the gamekeeper a nervous wreck by his constant involvement — or interference, as he saw it.

Sarah, in her bedroom, held a letter in her lap; a letter, the contents of which both thrilled and alarmed her. Life changing, that's how she saw it, more so than even the war had been for her — and, in some ways, more threatening, not only to her established way of life but also to that of her parents should she dare to reveal what it contained.

She got up from her chair and walked across the room to her wardrobe. Here she looked for a suitable outfit, something modern but not overly fashionable, something which would give the impression of a young lady embarking on a professional, responsible career.

Every garment she took out, though, seemed to be more representative of a lady of leisure. There was nothing here that came close to what she needed. She closed the doors and went back to her chair by the window.

She took up the letter again. She practically knew it by heart.

'We are pleased to inform you . . . '

The words were like nectar. She had never experienced that sensation of having achieved something by her own efforts, and based on her abilities and it gave her a warm feeling inside.

But it, likewise, sent a chill through her as she imagined the consequences should she take up the offer. Life, sometimes, seemed to be so complicated when it could be so simple, if it weren't for other people.

She returned to the issue of an outfit. She would have to go to town — to London town, and see what could be done, despite the rationing.

★　★　★

Sir Percy Fywell-Bennet was once again prowling around Merefield Hall. On this occasion, whether by chance or accident, Lord Trenton was not there to meet him, so it was left to Lady Patricia to accept his call.

The day being Tuesday, Sarah had decided to go into Shepham where the weekly market was taking place. Here, amongst the many stalls she was hoping to find material for her dressmaker to turn into an outfit suitable for her forthcoming position as a school secretary.

She'd decided in the end not to go to London. The thought of seeing the capital city still showing the scars of the war did not appeal to her, besides, with the rationing, she'd not fare better than anyone else in trying to get fitted out for work.

'If you've come here to see my husband then I'm afraid you've had a wasted journey.' Lady Patricia remained standing in the drawing-room as she addressed Sir Percy. By doing so she intended it to be clear that she would not be offering any hospitality to the man.

Fywell-Bennet was not so easily put off.

'That's not a problem, my lady. It's always a pleasure to spend time in your company ... and ... er ... Lady Sarah's.' He was looking round the room as he said this, as if Sarah might be hiding behind the furniture.

Lady Patricia soon dispelled that folly.

'My daughter is not at home, either.' She could not — would not — bring herself to use Sarah's name in this detestable man's company.

Again, Sir Percy was not to be put off, although, secretly he was seething.

'Never mind. I was hoping to have a word with you, anyway. May I?' He gestured to a nearby chair so that Lady Patricia felt she had no choice but to allow him, at the same time apprehensive as to what he could possibly have to say to her.

When she was seated herself, he began.

'As you may or not be aware, your husband and I have entered into an agreement, the result of which will be the happy union of Lady Sarah and myself in marriage.'

It was now Lady Patricia's turn to be angry, only, unlike Fywell-Bennet, she chose not to keep it to herself.

'I know nothing of the sort! Your presumption in such matters astonishes me. How dare you assume that my daughter would even consider such a thing?'

Sir Percy was both surprised and amused at the spirit the lady was showing.

'I can assure you it's no presumption. Just because Lord Trenton may not have discussed the finer details with you doesn't mean it's not going to happen.'

'And what does my daughter say to all this?'

Sir Percy raised an eyebrow.

'Do you mean she has not mentioned to you all the circumstances which has made my marrying her possible? I admit, ma'am, I am not a little surprised.'

'There are no circumstances!' Lady

Patricia insisted. 'My daughter is free to do as she likes, and that includes who she decides to marry, if that's what she wants.'

Sir Percy grinned in a most infuriating way, just like a Cheshire cat.

'I think you'll find, dear lady, that that decision has already been made for her.'

'My husband might be fooled by you but I am not. As I said, the only decision that can be made — if indeed it ever has to be — is one that my daughter, and my daughter alone, can make.' She stood up, perhaps a little too quickly before collapsing in a heap on to the carpeted floor.

Sir Percy only now stood up and for a few moments lingered over the still but breathing frame of Lady Patricia. How convenient, he was thinking, as the door opened and Sarah, totally unaware of what she was about to see, entered the room.

'Mummy!' she screamed, not acknowledging the presence of Fywell-Bennet, who was now standing some distance from the prostrate figure of Lady Patricia, as if to disown any responsibility for what had taken place.

But Sarah was in no doubt that he was in some way to blame.

'What have you done!' She was down on the floor herself now, cradling her mother's head in her arms. Lady Patricia remained unconscious, unresponsive as yet to all her daughter's frantic attempts to rouse her into life.

'We were just enjoying one another's company, and then she stood up and seemed to have a turn.'

The commotion had roused the below stairs staff, first Maisie the scullery maid and then Foster now entering the room.

'Call an ambulance!' Sarah called, without taking her eyes off her mother.

'Yes, call an ambulance. That's right. Just what I was about to do. Go on, hurry, hurry.' Sir Percy, struck by the seriousness of the situation and aware that anyone — and everyone — would think that he might possibly be the cause of it, took on a concerned yet responsible and caring attitude, driving Foster and Maisie out of the room with a rapid display of flapping arms.

'You'd better go, too,' Sarah said, in a threatening tone, 'and don't you ever come back here. I never want to see you again.'

'Very well, I can see you're upset, understandably so — but we will meet again, I can assure you.' And so, with his own air of menace, he hurried out of the room.

★ ★ ★

'An ambulance just went by,' Helen gasped, running in through the door of the Penfold cottage.

Mrs Penfold looked up from her chair where she'd been shelling the last of this year's peas.

'Which way?'

'Towards the Hall. What d'you think's happened, Mum?'

Mrs Penfold did not reply but,

138

instead, went out of the cottage and looked as far as she could up the private road which led to the Hall.

She felt anxious for all concerned up there, especially as, earlier in the day, she'd seen Sir Percy drive past in his sports car. It was not a good omen, and her apprehension prevented her from going back indoors and consulting her Tarot cards as she might have done in such circumstances.

But this was not the time or place. Even so, she felt a deep misgiving as an image of a prostrate Lady Patricia became as clear to her as if she was in the room where she actually lay.

She walked back slowly indoors. Helen was now in her chair, with Dime on her lap.

'Did you see anything?'

'No.'

Helen gave her mother a long, appraising look.

'You know who it's for, don't you?'

'I'm not sure, no.'

'Who d'you think it might be?' Helen

saw more of an adventure than a potential tragedy in what was taking place.

'I don't know, Helen. We'll just have to wait and see. Now jump up and take that dog with you so I can finish what I was doing.'

Sooner Rather than Later

The news soon spread round the village that an ambulance had been seen hurtling towards and then away from Merefield Hall.

There was much speculation as to who it might contain, but not even Jack Penfold or his son Robert were any wiser than the rest of them. They knew it couldn't be Lord Trenton, however, as Jack had been out with him at the time the ambulance arrived.

This left Lady Patricia or Sarah. Robert was aware that Fywell-Bennet had been at the Hall at the time, and the knowledge of it was adding to his concerns.

But there was nothing he could do to find out any more; he was as dependent as the villagers on learning something from any member of the household staff who might happen to be in the village.

If something had happened to Sarah

he would never forgive himself. If that swine Fywell-Bennet had done anything to harm her he'd make him pay for it.

But, even as these things were going through his mind, he was conscious of the fact that he was just a nobody with absolutely no right to involve himself in matters relating to the Hall.

Sarah remained at her mother's bedside in the private room of the cottage hospital, keeping a vigil, waiting for her mother to regain consciousness, to come back to life — to her.

The doctors seemed to think she had suffered a mild stroke, activated — possibly — by a sudden and unexpected surge in adrenalin. They were cautiously optimistic that she would make a recovery of sorts which, in the circumstances, was the only straw of comfort that Sarah could cling on to.

Lord Trenton visited once or twice, but seemed disturbed and uncomfortable by the sight of his wife in such a fragile, lifeless-looking state. As long as Sarah remained with her he felt justified in not staying. He loved his wife and could not even contemplate a situation where she might not be there.

He could accept death in nature and in livestock. He had indeed been a witness and participant in both but, ever since Michael died, he'd closed his eyes and heart to the prospect of losing anyone else.

Sarah, of her own volition, talked and read to Lady Patricia; it did her good in that it offered a distraction to all that was taking place.

And finally she was rewarded.

It was around about the fourth day that Lady Patricia responded to her daughter. Sarah had been giving her all sorts of trivial details about this and that and nothing in particular when she suddenly saw her mother's eyes slowly open.

She swiftly rose from her chair and moved closer, taking Lady Patricia's hand in hers and smiling.

'Oh, Mummy, dear Mummy, you're awake.'

Weak as she was, Lady Patricia was able to squeeze Sarah's hand in response whilst at the same time effecting a smile of her own.

'What happened?' Her voice was faint and frail but clear enough for Sarah to understand.

'You collapsed, Mummy darling, but you're all right now. You're in the hospital and being taken very good care of.' She was stroking her mother's brow as she spoke, feeling relieved and yet tearful at the same time.

'I'm very tired. Have I been asleep?'

'You have, yes, and for quite a while.'

'What happened?'

'I'm not sure. I came home and found you collapsed on the drawing-room floor, with that dreadful man, Sir Percy Fywell-Bennet standing over you. I thought he'd caused you some harm.'

Lady Patricia shook her head slowly.

'I don't remember. Why was he there?'

'I don't know. I'd imagined he'd come to speak with you.' Sarah was feeling a little alarmed at her mother's lack of memory. She slowly rose, releasing her hold on Lady Patricia's hand. 'I'm just going to go and find a doctor, I won't be long. Try to stay awake, Mummy.'

She returned a few minutes later with Mr Shephard, a consultant who specialised in neurological disorders. He showed great efficiency as he examined Lady Patricia, taking her pulse and temperature and peering into her eyes with the aid of a small pencil torch.

'How is she?'

Mr Shephard turned from his patient. His expression remained serious as he addressed Sarah.

'We had thought, initially, that your mother had had a stroke, but all the tests we've carried out suggest that she may have angina.'

'Angina! Does that mean she was having a heart attack?'

'Not necessarily. During the war I came upon a number of cases similar to this where the patient suddenly collapses. It's a sort of coping mechanism in a contrary way. They find that they cannot deal with the situation they are faced with so everything shuts down.'

'What about her memory? She says she cannot remember what happened leading up to it.'

'Was anyone else present at the time?'

Sarah shifted uneasily.

'There was a visitor with her at the time.'

'Perhaps you should ask him . . . or her. As for the memory, I don't think any long-term harm has occurred but we'll be keeping her in for a while yet, just to be on the safe side.' He looked closely at Sarah, noting the fatigue and anxiety etched on her face.

'You should take care of yourself,' he said, smiling. 'Go home, get some rest. Afterwards you can saddle up that horse of yours and get some fresh air into your lungs. You won't be any use to your family if you're always exhausted.

'Your mother's in safe hands here and you can visit whenever you like, but for now it's home and bed for you, young lady.'

The news had finally filtered through to the village and estate that it was Lady Patricia who'd been the one taken off in the ambulance.

For Robert it had come, initially, as a huge relief, swiftly followed by an overwhelming feeling of guilt, that his first reaction should have been so inconsiderate. Sarah — and Lord Trenton — must be worried sick, but, again, he could think of no way that he could see Sarah and offer comfort and support.

'They say she's on the mend,' Jack Penfold said to his wife, late one morning when he'd been out on the heathland with his master.

'That's good news. Will she be home soon, do you think?'

'Can't say. Lady Sarah's been going to the hospital every day now for near enough a fortnight, but the viscount seems to find any excuse not to go.'

'It would be too upsetting for the poor man. He's much better making himself useful around the estate.'

Jack Penfold gave his wife a look

suggesting a difference of opinion on the matter, but he said nothing, getting up from his chair and heading for the door.

'Where's the boy?' he asked, turning.

Elizabeth Penfold sighed.

'If you're talking about your son, he's not a boy, he's a grown man. And I think he went for a walk.'

'He needs to walk into the Labour Exchange and get himself a job — a proper job,' he added as he walked out of the house, this being his own response to the fact that Robert was now qualified to take up a teaching post.

Robert had indeed been on a walk. He was still on it in fact, although, for the moment he'd paused to take in the view. Not the view of natural landscape, where much was in evidence regarding flora and fauna.

No, on this occasion he was more interested in the progress of the construction of the new estate, and in particular the primary school which, he could now see, was nearing completion.

The square lines and red brick of the building would not win its architect a knighthood, but its very existence — its modernity, its face to the future — filled Robert with a great sense of anticipation.

Things were changing. People would have decent, sanitised housing, there would be a public library as well as a school. There were even plans for both a social club and a church.

But again, Robert's attention returned to the school, and the job he hoped to have there. He'd already been for one interview and, today, had received notification that the education committee wanted to see him again.

It was all good, all promising, and it would be even better if he could have shared his hopes and aspirations with Sarah. But, of course, at the present time that wasn't possible and he felt again a pang of guilt at his own apparent selfishness.

Not that she would have been too interested, anyway, he considered. She'd never been in favour of the estate and had made a point of avoiding the place once she'd witnessed the grubbing out of the fruit trees.

Robert sighed. He didn't know what to do any more. He loved Sarah and he believed she loved him but it wasn't getting them anywhere. And now time was making its mark.

Decisions about the future were going to have to be made, sooner rather than later, with or without Sarah. And it wouldn't be easy, for either of them.

He turned from the view, heading back towards Westmoor wood. As he did he noticed some of the many flowers that bloomed hereabouts showing themselves in amongst the grass or at the foot of trees and hedges. And in that moment he understood completely what some might gain and others lose.

A Dream Come True

Lady Patricia finally returned home, brought back in the more conventional form of the chauffeur-driven limousine. She was accompanied by Sarah who seemed to be her constant companion these days.

The staff, such as they were in these enlightened post-war days, all stood out on the gravelled driveway to await the viscountess's arrival.

It was noticed but obviously not remarked upon that Lady Patricia appeared older and more fragile than before. But her manner was, if anything, even more sweet natured as she acknowledged and greeted her servants.

It was arranged that she would confine herself to her own bedroom for the present time. A spacious apartment with large casement windows offering both good light and view, it would allow her to fully recover at her own pace, without any interruptions or matters to concern her with.

Sarah, for her part, would be in charge of her general welfare, keeping her company and helping with some of her less personal toilette.

In this way the days passed peacefully, but there was still no clue as to what incident had caused her collapse. She was aware that Fywell-Bennet had been in the room at the time but, other than that, her mind was a blank.

What was a little more disturbing was her reaction to a large bouquet of flowers which arrived shortly after her homecoming. They were from Fywell-Bennet, carrying a gracious and considerate message for her well being. Lady Patricia seemed pleased by them, wanting them placed on a table by the window.

'How very thoughtful of him,' she said, admiring the bouquet in its chosen place. Sarah chose to stay silent. It was too soon to be quarrelling, she must let it go, for now.

★ ★ ★

By the beginning of August, Lady Patricia was well enough to come downstairs and, on days when the weather behaved as a summer's day should, she would sit in the rose garden where sunlight and privacy all added to her recovery.

Sarah, reasonably satisfied that her mother could be left for a while — having made sure staff members would be keeping a discreet eye on her — decided it was time to give Cymbeline some much-needed exercise.

Lord Trenton had been keeping the animal exercised by allowing one of the more trustworthy and responsible stable lads to ride him every other day, mostly within sight of the Hall.

This had kept the thoroughbred 'steady' but it was no real substitute for having Sarah take him out.

After a heady gallop along the boundary edge of the formal parkland Sarah didn't even need to turn his head towards Westmoor wood, where soon they were back up on the central edge. Here, as was usual, Sarah stopped to look down at her beloved home.

To see it you would think that nothing had changed, but despite it appearing to exist in its own time capsule, there was much happening that was beginning to encroach, and which, given time, could totally undermine its very foundations.

'Penny for them?'

Both Sarah and Cymbeline turned their heads at the same time, the horse giving a small whinny of appreciative greeting.

'Robert!'

'Is that all you've got to say?' Robert said, moving out of the shadows. He put his hand to Cymbeline's nose, not certain — again — how Sarah might react if he were to take her hand. He felt that now, whenever they met — which was always, it seemed, by chance and not arrangement — they were having to start all over again, they could not maintain any sort of progress.

And always, at the back of Robert's mind was the fact that Sarah had not agreed to marry him when he'd asked her.

He didn't know where he stood with her any more. Perhaps she only ever wanted him as a lover. After all, the war had encouraged an attitude of *laissez faire*. Five years of living with the prospect of death had both hardened people's resolve and softened their moral outlook on life.

And why would Sarah be any different? Except that, in his heart of hearts, he knew that with her it wasn't the case. All these troubling thoughts were never far away, though. Even now as he stroked Cymbeline's nose, he was tormenting himself with them.

'Are you getting down? Shall I help?'

'No,' she said, more abruptly than she intended. 'I cannot stay. I must get back to Mu . . . my mother.'

He was aware of the change to a formal address of Lady Patricia, and it hurt. Hurt because it was the strongest indication yet that they were drifting apart, that he had no right or claim to her heart or her position in society. Not for the first time he felt humiliated by her seemingly cold manner. Know your place, boy, he could hear his father say. She's not for you.

The situation still demanded, however, a few common courtesies.

'How is Lady Patricia?'

'She's slowly getting better, thank you. As I said, I must get back, she'll be wondering where I've got to.'

Robert took his hand from the horse's head and came alongside Sarah. Looking up at her he felt an ache — a longing — that he thought he could not survive, but he kept it hidden as he spoke.

'We're bound to come across each other from time to time.' He hesitated. 'So I hope we can remain . . . civil to one another.'

He was going to say 'friends' but that was not actually a compromise he was willing in all sincerity to make.

'What do you mean, be civil? I don't understand.'

'Well, clearly your feelings towards me have changed . . . '

'It's everything else that has changed, Robert, and I have no control over that.'

For a moment he felt a faint hope.

'What do you mean?'

'I mean that feelings — yours or mine — are of no consequence, not now, not ever, maybe. And there's nothing either of us can do about it, so what is the point?'

He could see that her eyes were moistening, that the words she was saying were hurting her as much as him. He put a hand up and she, to his surprise, took it.

'We're here, we're alive, that is the point, Sarah.'

She looked down at him; their eyes became fixed on each other.

'Help me down,' she said finally.

It was a familiar scenario, him with his arms outstretched, gently helping

Sarah to the ground. Down to my level, came into his head, uninvited.

This time, though, there was no passionate embrace. Sarah simply put her arms around Robert, pressing her face into his chest. What she wanted from him was comfort, support, understanding.

'Mummy's not right,' she whispered.

Robert pulled her away.

'Not right? In what way?'

Sarah sighed.

'Physically she's doing very well. Mr Shephard's really pleased with her progress. It's just . . . in herself, she doesn't seem the same.'

'How is she different?'

'It's hard to say.' Letting go of Cymbeline's reins Sarah and Robert both sat down and leaned against a beech tree which offered both shade and concealment. Again Robert took Sarah's hand in his as she continued talking.

'She seems to have lost that . . . that fire she once had. Her spirit seems to have gone.'

'It could be the medication she's on — that can sometimes have an effect.'

'I suppose so. But it worries — frightens — me and I'm afraid to leave her for too long in case she just, well, drifts away.'

They were both silent for a while, each one dwelling on what Sarah had just said. Cymbeline turned his head to look at them briefly before returning to grazing the sparse grass at his feet.

Sarah leaned her head on Robert's shoulder.

'I should be getting back.' Her voice had gone very quiet and when Robert shifted his position very slightly, very gently, he could see that she had fallen asleep. He chose not to wake her. For the time being at least there was peace between them. A dream come true.

Good News and Bad News

Lord Trenton lived by the maxim whereby if he didn't like or agree with something he could remove it from his presence. However, that was all well and good with matters where his authority was not to be questioned, but with other, less obvious things, he struggled.

He'd visited Lady Patricia only when he absolutely had to. He'd struggled to accept that she was ill, ill enough to be in hospital, and even when she returned home her removal — even though of her own choosing — to a separate bed chamber relieved him of any responsibility of care, other than ensuring that Sarah, or anyone else, was in attendance to her needs.

In this attitude he found he had a surprising ally in the shape of Sir Percy Fywell-Bennet, who was nearly now as close as Lord Trenton's own shadow.

But instead of resenting his company, the viscount was rather glad of it.

He could see a way forward, the future, one that would benefit not only his daughter — when she eventually came to accept the idea — but the estate and family name in general.

Fywell-Bennet might not have been his first choice but circumstances had persuaded him that it would solve for ever the problem of Sarah and the Penfold boy's unwanted attentions.

He was unaware that this would also solve most of Sir Percy's problems too, if only for the immediate future. He'd been the subject of more demands for payment and, in some cases, the tone of these letters was becoming threatening. So he was having to spend more time 'working on the old man', as he'd told one of his fellow gambling cronies, in order to get what he wanted.

Fortunately, from his point of view, Lady Patricia was out of the picture. A good thing too, he thought, knowing that she could see through his shallow ambitions regarding marriage to her daughter.

The two men were standing together, overlooking the extensive heathland where the first shoot of the season would be taking place in less than a fortnight. Sir Percy had been showering Lord Trenton with compliments regarding the number of birds there would be, and the stunning setting for the occasion.

'Let's hope the twelfth proves to be as glorious as today, my lord.'

The weather was indeed hot and, under his check tweed flat cap, Fywell-Bennet was perspiring in a most ungentlemanly way.

Lord Trenton, despite all that was complicating his life at present, always found being out of doors lifted his spirits and tended to make things seem better.

Perhaps it was because he was able to physically distance himself from these affairs or perhaps, at this present time, it was the prospect of a number of distinguished guns shooting on his estate which gave him a feeling of self-fulfilment, something he had not experienced for some time.

Although he harboured certain misgivings concerning the suitability of Sir Percy as a son-in-law, fuelled by various rumours that, despite the baronet's best efforts, had reached his ears, his present 'out of doors' mood lifted his spirits to a point where he wasn't seeing things as clearly as he might.

Sir Percy Fywell-Bennet was taking every advantage of the situation, ingratiating himself with the viscount. He had already extracted an invitation to the first day's shooting which meant he would certainly be a guest at that evening's supper where Sarah must, by protocol, attend, especially as she was deputising for her mother in the day-to-day running of the Hall.

She would be a captive audience, and he would remind her then of her responsibilities not only to her own family but to the future security and welfare of Jack Penfold and his 'tribe', as he thought of them.

'There should a good bag on the day. Penfold's done well with the birds. We've suffered very little loss by way of foxes and poachers. Yes, he's a good man.'

Fywell-Bennet did not care for Lord Trenton's ringing endorsement of the gamekeeper. He needed him to see them as a threat to the honourable name and reputation of his Lordship.

'I wouldn't say the same of his son,' he said, with malicious intent. 'He's still sniffing around young Sarah, you know.'

Lord Trenton turned to face Sir Percy.

'How is that so?' he demanded. 'I strictly forbade the pair of them to continue with their . . . their . . . liaison. What do you know about this?' There was that steely glint in the viscount's eyes and, in his manner and tone of voice, he seemed to be implying that Fywell-Bennet should have come to him sooner with this revelation. Either that or he was lying to gain his own advantage.

'Only what my servants and the locals have been hearing, my lord. I'm sure all it would take is another word from you — to the Lady Sarah — and it will put a stop to their shenanigans once and for all. I could speak to Penfold junior if it might help at all.'

The viscount considered this for a moment.

'Very well. But just you make it perfectly clear that I will not tolerate any more of his underhand behaviour or there will be serious consequences.'

Satisfied that he had restored the status quo back in his favour, Sir Percy soon made his excuses to leave. But instead of going directly home he called in at the Hall, demanding to see Sarah.

Despite her dislike and distrust of the man, Sarah nevertheless came from the drawing-room, where Lady Patricia was continuing her convalescence, to meet him. It was only after he'd spoken and then left that she'd wished with all her heart that she'd avoided the encounter.

Two letters came the following morning to the Lodge.

'They're both for you, Robert,' his mother said. One has been hand delivered.' She didn't add that she knew who it was from. She didn't have to, they both knew.

Robert took them. The other missive looked much more official, typewritten and addressing him in his capacity as an officer in the RAF, even going so far as to add the DSO after his name.

He took them both to his room. Being aware of his mother's psychic powers he imagined she'd know their contents more or less at the same time as he would be reading them if he stayed in the same room as her.

In his bedroom he opened the official-looking letter first. It was from the head of the regional education committee offering him a position as a probationer in the boys' section of the nearly completed primary school on

Lord Trenton's formerly owned land.

It was exactly what he'd been hoping for but the pleasure was being dulled by the apprehension that was growing within him on looking now at the other letter lying near him on the bed.

He not only knew who it was from but had a fair idea of what it might contain, and it wouldn't be good news. When their love affair first began they never needed to write to one another.

They could, back then, meet without ever arousing any suspicion regarding the state of their relationship. After all, they'd grown up together and were always in each other's company, so much so that no-one thought it unusual to see them together.

But since Michael's death and the changing attitude of Lord Trenton, coupled with the more recent sinister intrusion by Sir Percy Fywell-Bennet, they'd been forced to resort to subterfuge, and letters, most of which had not contained — from Sarah, anyway — good news.

Best get it over with, he told himself,

and opened the envelope. As he imagined, it did not contain anything from which he might take a shred of comfort.

'That vile man, Fywell-Bennet, has been making more threats to me but against you,' he read. 'He seems to have taken in my father to such an extent that I'm frightened he will act on the man's say-so. That is why, Robert, we have to stop seeing each other. I have my mother to deal with, which, with the running of the household, is taking away most of my free time anyway.

'And I cannot be always worrying that we could be jeopardising your family's welfare and job security by our own self interest. It has taken me a long time to write this; it did not come easy, but it has to be for the best, for all our sakes. Sarah.'

What actually hurt Robert the most was the ending, where she'd simply signed herself off as Sarah. It was as if what they had been to each other had counted for nothing. But then he realised she was only trying to make it plain that their relationship, such as it was, was at an end.

When he sat there, thinking about it, he could only now remember the clandestine nature of it all. They had never, officially, been on a date. It had always been out of sight of others, hastily arranged meetings in or about the less peopled areas of the estate. That was no way to show someone you loved them.

He saw himself as a coward. Even the humiliating scenario with Fywell-Bennet made him look weak. Why hadn't he struck him? He certainly deserved it, but had he done so it would have caused more damage to himself and, more importantly, his family, than to anyone else.

It still made him look ineffectual. It gave the appearance of someone not caring enough to do whatever required for the sake of his love.

Sarah had probably seen that, too, his weakness, and his total unsuitability as anything other than a conditional friend. She had unconsciously closed ranks with Fywell-Bennet, even though she claimed to loathe him.

Love doesn't conquer all, Robert

thought bitterly. Class does.

The sound of his father bellowing his name brought Robert swiftly out of his unhappy thoughts. He ran down the stairs, his heart thumping.

'What is it? What's happened?'

Mrs Penfold looked up from her sewing, a sympathetic expression on her face.

'There's nothing wrong, dear. Your father has a favour to ask you.'

Jack Penfold, who'd been leaning against the kitchen table, turned and gave his wife a withering look.

'I ask no favours of anyone,' he told her. He turned back to his son. 'There's work for you as a beater if you want it. Same rates as last year.' He waited briefly and impatiently for a response. When none immediately came, he moved menacingly towards his son. 'Well? Do you want it or not?'

Robert quickly recovered his composure.

'I hardly think Lord Trenton will want me anywhere near his shoot.'

Jack Penfold sneered.

'He's hardly going to notice the likes of you, you're nobody to him, especially as you've come to your senses over Lady Sarah. So, are you up for it?'

Robert was aware that, despite the bluff and bluster, his father really did want him involved. And, although he may not have come to his senses, Sarah assuredly had, which meant he was free to do as he pleased — with a clear conscience.

'Yes, I'm up for it.'

There was no need for further discussion, so Jack Penfold turned and left. Mrs Penfold looked at her son who seemed not to know where to place his gaze.

'Come and sit down, love. There's tea in the pot.'

Seated opposite each other at the kitchen table, Robert said nothing whilst his mother poured the tea. There was a silence between them that was full of questions and no answers.

'There you are, Robert.' She pushed the cup and saucer towards him. 'Do you want any cake — or a scone, maybe? I baked a batch this morning.'

'No, thanks, I'm not really hungry.'

'I'm not prying, love, but I guessed from the handwriting that the letter was from Sarah, and I can tell from your face that it didn't have good news.'

'You could say that.' He shifted uncomfortably in his chair, feeling awkward at the distress he was needlessly causing his mother. 'I did have some good news, though.'

He took the official-looking document from his pocket and passed it over to her. 'Read that.'

'I'll have to get my glasses.' She went to get up but Robert waved her down and read her the contents, himself. She beamed with pride and came round the table and kissed the top of his head.

'You're not only clever you're a good man, Robert,' she said, conveying both her pride in his achievement and the strength of love she had for him in what she knew was a difficult and troubling time.

Beyond the Stars

Lady Patricia's health and recovery were benefiting from the continuous warm August weather. She would spend most afternoons in the rose garden where she could enjoy sun or shade. Although the roses themselves were past their best blooming, there were still enough flowers to give off a subtle aroma to act like a healing balm.

Her memory was slowly returning but it could still not piece together the immediate precursor to her collapse, other than that her feelings regarding Sir Percy Fywell-Bennet were starting to revert to the way they had been prior to that day.

As her strength grew so too did her concern over Sarah's welfare. She had taken on most, if not all, of Lady Patricia's responsibilities at a cost to her own health and well being.

She knew, too, that her husband's strictures were causing Sarah to have to come to terms with what the viscount thought was best for all concerned.

It was just that there was something about Sir Percy which aroused suspicion and repulsion in her. Odious, that was the word. He was an odious man and she was suddenly certain that he had, in some way, been the catalyst in her collapse.

Having time on her hands was becoming tedious. Lady Patricia was starting to feel not only stronger but resolved to do a little digging.

The first day of the shoot arrived, the glorious twelfth lived up to its name in all respects and by the end of the day all those invited guests were well pleased with their results.

Robert had taken part as a beater, and it brought out an unusual reaction in his father, a sort of wordless appreciation. It was difficult to pinpoint, but there was something in his manner towards him that suggested possibly relief in that, for

Jack Penfold at least, past events would now be just that, something consigned to history. Today was good, and tomorrow would be better.

Maybe it was one or all of these things or maybe the gamekeeper was just relieved that everything — from first light onwards — had gone smoothly. Whatever it was, Robert was pleased that he and his father were able to be amicable to one another. That at least was one less thing to be concerned about.

Around 12.30 a horse-drawn wagon came to a clearing cut in the heather. On board were one or two staff, including Cook, and around and about them was food ready prepared for the guests' luncheon. Walking behind were the domestic servants whose job it would be to serve the food.

A second wagon, following, brought with it a number of trestle tables and chairs for the luncheon guests. For the beaters there was the long walk back to the kitchen to partake of their own less lavish fare provided by Lord Trenton.

Not wishing to appear standoffish, Robert took part in this 'tradition' where a distance was maintained between the upper and lower orders. In the past he'd never thought of it in these terms — had just enjoyed the participation with others from the Hall and the village — but today it was making him feel like he was a peasant, although he could not blame anyone else but himself for that.

It was the consciousness of the separation of his life from Sarah, from the realisation that — even if she was willing — he could never in a million years ever hope to offer her anything like the life and privilege she enjoyed.

Fywell-Bennet had been watching Robert off and on during this time, but for him there was still the lingering doubt — an uneasy uncertainty — that there might still be something between the upstart and Sarah.

Sarah herself was still showing no sign of accepting Sir Percy as a possible suitor, despite what he imagined were his best efforts. Actually though, his best efforts were more consistently being directed at Sarah's father — increasingly so in the light of what he'd heard concerning Lady Patricia and her gradual recovery from her fall.

Should she fully recollect what had taken place that day prior to her collapse, it would show Fywell-Bennet in a very unflattering light and that simply would not do.

Sarah remained at the Hall during all this. Lady Patricia was indeed a lot better which was good but it made Sarah feel a bit of a fraud — a coward? — as she still continued to use her mother's convalescence as an excuse for avoiding the company of others. This evening, however, there would be no place to hide.

'I think I should like to be in attendance this evening, for a while, dear,' Lady Patricia had told her. Sarah could not deny that her mother was indeed fit enough for such an undertaking, and it would have been dishonest to say otherwise. But the prospect alarmed her.

She would have no reason, now, not to be there herself thus enabling Sir Percy to speak to her.

'That's good, Mummy. I'm sure everyone will be pleased to see you.'

*　　*　　*

There were quite a number of guests staying at the Hall. Along with the servants each had brought with them, the place, large as it was, was bursting at the seams.

Lord Trenton was in his element. He thoroughly enjoyed hosting such a manly event. But Sarah found it intimidating, especially as so many eyes would be on her, being the feminine interest to the party, so to speak.

That was why she attempted to maintain such close contact with her mother who, unlike Sarah, seemed to be thoroughly relishing the limelight. She moved amongst the guests with all her former grace and charm, and Sarah, despite being aware of a particular pair of eyes continually following her around the room, felt pleased and proud to see her on such good form.

Even Lord Trenton appeared to be proudly aware — if not relieved — to have his wife back within the social circle. All in all, the evening was being a success.

With the vast majority of guests being men there was no need for any sort of musical entertainment. A few card schools were starting up at variously strategically placed baize covered tables.

Sir Percy, unable to help himself, had become distracted enough by the prospect of winning some money. He never considered he might lose, despite overwhelming evidence to the contrary and had allowed his eyes to dwell on an altogether different queen of hearts.

Much to everyone's surprise — not least, Sarah's — Lady Patricia disengaged herself from her daughter and approached the table where Sir Percy, amongst others, sat.

'May I join you?'

Such was the astonishment etched on each of the now standing players that no-one, at first, managed to respond.

'Why of course, my lady.' Sir Percy was the first to recover from the shock of her request and hastily pulled out a chair for her.

'Thank you. Now, what are we playing?'

Sarah, cut loose, began to stray, wandering aimlessly on her own, engaging in little snippets of inane conversation. The fact was, she was bored — bored stiff. The smoky, masculine atmosphere of the room she found unbearable.

Making sure no-one saw, she slipped out through the French windows on to the terrace where the evening sky and the silent stillness of everything calmed her mood. She looked heavenward, recognising the constellations growing ever more visible as the darkness descended.

She held up a hand, tracing the shapes of those she knew. Then her arm dropped but she still fixed her gaze upwards as she thought of Michael, now beyond that sky which, for so long, had been his battleground. It made her feel proud and sad at the same time.

When I am old you will still be young, she thought. For some strange reason this thought gave her comfort as she considered the things that he would not have to face, that no-one ever speaks of.

Apart from not growing old he would not know the heartache and despair she had experienced.

Her thoughts turned now towards Robert. She could not see the lodge house where the Penfold family lived but she looked, anyway, in its direction. Robert, too, had been up in the sky, the same as Michael, but he had been one of the lucky ones, a fact which her father still seemed to resent.

Yet, who at that age could honestly wish to put their life at risk, day in day out, for years. This was what Lord Trenton seemed to forget, that Robert took the same risks as her brother and was prepared to die, like Michael, for the cause.

That he hadn't was something for which Sarah would always be grateful. It was just that, sometimes, when she was feeling as low as she was right now, she could see that life was offering little to make her feel it had all been worth it.

'There you are. I've been hunting high and low for you, my girl.'

Sarah turned to see her father, a silhouette against the light coming from the open french windows. He was standing taller than she'd seen him for some time.

The success of the shoot, his wife's recovery, plus other things which she might not be fully aware of, had all combined to restore his good humour and stature. She smiled as she walked towards him.

'Is everything all right?'

'Fine, fine.' He chuckled. 'Your mother is showing the men — especially Sir Percy — how to win at cards.'

'Has she won some money?'

'More than that. Fywell-Bennet found himself not only on the losing end but financially embarrassed as a result.'

'What does that mean?' They were back in the room. Sarah looked all around and, to her relief, could not see the repugnant figure of the man in question.

'It means he's had to write her an IOU.'

Sarah was shocked.

'How much did she win off him?'

'Oh, not a great deal. It's just that he wasn't expecting it, and wasn't carrying much cash on him. He's gone off home in a bit of a huff.

'Anyway, enough of that. Your mother's looking a bit tired after all the excitement and she ought to go to bed. Perhaps you'll persuade her.'

Sarah followed Lord Trenton back into the drawing-room and, on finding Lady Patricia, had little trouble persuading her to retire.

'Yes, I am rather tired but I've thoroughly enjoyed myself.' She had a mischievous twinkle in her eye which Sarah wasn't quite sure how to interpret.

'I hear you've been winning at the cards,' Sarah remarked, as she guided her mother between the guests, out of the room and back upstairs to her bedroom.

'It was fun. I think Sir Percy was particularly miffed. He's of the old school. He thinks ladies just arrange flowers, go shopping and organise meals.'

Sarah said nothing, simply smiling at these remarks. Once Lady Patricia was in bed, she bent to kiss her goodnight.

'Sleep well, Mummy.'

Lady Patricia held on to her daughter, an earnest expression now on her face.

'My memory of my fall, or rather what happened just before I collapsed, has been slowly coming back. That man is no good, and you must be careful, Sarah. Don't do anything your heart doesn't want you to.'

Sarah frowned.

'What do you mean?'

'We live in a new age. The old order is going. Don't be left behind because of what others might want.' She smiled at her daughter and stroked her face.

'It's your life, darling — it belongs to you.'

She sat up slightly and kissed Sarah's forehead. Sarah returned her smile but her mind was in a turmoil.

Worlds Apart

Sir Percy Fywell-Bennet was in his usual ill temper as he paced up and down across the threadbare carpet of his own drawing-room. He was still seething over the humiliation he'd been subjected to the previous evening, not only the fact that he'd lost all his money to a woman but the fact that he'd had to make out an IOU in her favour, all in front of the other smirking players.

'You rang, sir?'

The door had gently opened and Watkins the general dogsbody slipped into the room.

'I did indeed,' Sir Percy snapped, 'about five minutes ago.' He gave the unfortunate Watkins a withering look, then sighed. 'Watkins, I want to know what further news you have on that lout, Robert Penfold, the one who's been sniffing round my fiancée.'

Watkins managed to restrain the look of surprise which that last comment had had on him. He'd no idea things had reached this point, so he made an instant decision to censor the information he'd received concerning Robert and Sarah.

'It's my belief, sir, that the young lady has severed all connections with the young man in question, and that you should not be troubled further on his account.'

Fywell-Bennet turned away from his servant, so as to conceal the smug grin appearing on his face. This was good news indeed, and, as long as the mother kept her nose out, he shouldn't have any trouble making Lord Trenton fix a date for their forthcoming nuptials.

There was just the matter of the confounded IOU. It had shown him in a poor light. Drat the woman! Somehow, in order to save face, he would have to find the money to pay Lady Patricia back which could mean appealing to one of his many creditors yet again, not something he relished.

Still, he reflected, it would only put him temporarily further into debt. Once he was safely wedded to the daughter, it would be their money which would be paying his debts.

'Get me my coat, man. I've got business to attend to.'

★ ★ ★

Sarah, assured that her mother was a lot better, allowed her curiosity to get the better of her regarding the new estate being built on her father's former orchard.

Giving both herself and her parents the excuse that Cymbeline needed exercising, she took the horse along a less familiar pathway, towards where the new houses and school would eventually stand.

She still had the letter — and the secret — from the education committee offering her the position of secretary for that selfsame school and, although, now, she doubted she would take it up, she wanted to see for herself how far advanced all the building work was proceeding.

But as she got nearer, a familiar figure came into view — someone she wanted and didn't want to meet. He was standing with his back to her, also seeing for himself, it appeared, how the work was progressing.

She tried to silently turn Cymbeline, in order to go back the way they'd come, but the horse, also recognising Robert, held firm and let out a loud whinny which caught Robert's attention.

There was nothing now for it but to continue towards him, even though he hadn't made any gesture of acknowledgement towards Sarah. But Cymbeline pressed on regardless and on reaching him nuzzled his nose into Robert's amused face.

'Why hello, stranger,' he said — to Cymbeline — not intending any insinuation by it. Sarah, however, did take it personally and felt her cheeks burn. Robert looked up at her, a puzzled expression on his face.

'What brings you this way?'

Sarah looked past him to where work on the new estate was developing but she needed to get closer still in order to see anything.

'I just was wondering how far they've got with the building.'

'Me too. But we need to go along the path a bit further. Are you coming?'

Sarah wasn't sure what she should do. If someone saw her here — with Robert — and in this proximity with the new estate it might cause them both trouble — again.

But at the same time, having come this far, she was determined to discover what sort of environment she might be working in.

Having given it some thought, Sarah now dismounted and led Cymbeline along the narrow track with Robert leading the way.

As they drew nearer they could both hear the sounds of industry ahead, and once it was in view they stopped to take in all that now covered the land where only a matter of months ago orchards had stood. Sarah gave out a muted gasp at what she saw.

Houses had sprung up everywhere, along with a church, a modest parade of shops and, at its heart almost, the school.

There was still plenty of work going on, but it was the finishing touches, the finer details, that were now being attended to. A pair of steamrollers were moving slowly to and fro across the newly laid tarmac of the roads which linked avenue to avenue, driveway to driveway.

Landscape gardeners were planting trees and laying turf with others behind, with hoses, watering it all in. Robert witnessed it all with an almost childlike excitement. To him it epitomised what the war had ultimately been about, victory for the common man, woman and child all encapsulated in a scene such as this, a decent way of life, everyone's entitlement.

He secretly rejoiced in the fact that he would be a part of it, increasing

children's potential through the knowledge that education would have to
offer.

Sarah remained silent. After the
initial shock of what she'd seen, she
began to understand what Robert had
always meant by the things he'd said.

Despite the rawness and redness of
the architecture she, too, could see a
future here. The houses, the school, the
shops, and the church all symbolised a
belief in that future. For the first time
since the development had been given
the go-ahead, she unknowingly shared
Robert's enthusiasm for it all.

'What do you think? I don't suppose
you approve.'

There was a coldness in his tone that
both shocked and upset Sarah. It was as
if he had decided that the best course of
action was indifference. That way,
nobody got hurt.

But she was hurt and was finding it
difficult to stand in such close proximity to Robert, knowing — or believing,
anyway — that his feelings towards her

could have cooled to such a dispassion-
ate degree.

For his part, Robert was feeling as
uncomfortable as Sarah, but the only
way to keep the lid on his emotions was
to maintain a distance, both physically
as well as emotionally.

But it was hard. So much of him
yearned to reach out to Sarah and take
her in his arms as before, even though
he knew it was no longer possible to do
so.

He must move on and look towards a
different future than he had once hoped
for. And he realised that it was here,
below him, in the new estate where his
own future lay, not amongst the titled
elite — the rich man in his castle
— when he was so obviously the poor
man at his gate. No, better to accept his
place and try to make the best of it.

What he didn't realise was that Sarah
was having as much trouble herself
knowing where she stood in this new,
post-war, ever-changing world. Attitudes were altering, her own included,

but family was still very important even if their own attitudes were looking ever more outdated.

'I'm surprised at how much has been done . . . so many houses.'

'Does it upset you to see your father's orchards being built on?' Robert's voice had a softer edge to it as he asked the question. He could still understand how it must be hard for her to accept it all.

Sarah thought for a moment.

'No,' she said, a more confident tone evident in her voice. 'I can see it is for the best — for everyone.'

Robert smiled.

'I'm glad you see it that way. I can understand how difficult it must be for you — and your parents — to come to terms with it.'

Sarah stiffened. She didn't like being 'lumped in' with her parents over this. It made her seem rather old-fashioned, something she hadn't considered before. Traditional, yes, but also not inflexible in her outlook on life — modern life — in general.

'I think some changes are necessary.' She knew she was sounding almost patronising in her response but, really, it was Robert's fault for making her seem like a Luddite, as if hers was a family of dinosaurs.

She saw no point in continuing this conversation so, politely — formally — excusing herself, she turned Cymbeline back down the path from the direction they'd travelled.

Robert, aware that Sarah was somehow upset by their meeting, was dithering as to what to do. Better perhaps to leave things as they were. After all their affair, such as it was, was definitely now dead in the water. But he felt bad that they should be parting on not the best of terms.

'Sarah, wait!'

Follow Your Heart

'Where have you been, dear?'

Sarah, having returned from her unintended meeting with Robert, had put Cymbeline back into his paddock and gone in search of her mother. She didn't at first see her as she entered the rose garden. The continuing sweltering heat of August was becoming oppressive and Lady Patricia had moved into a more shaded area, not immediately visible.

'Oh, Mummy, there you are.' Sarah moved across the parched grass and sat in the other deck chair.

Lady Patricia had seen Sarah, though, and had noted that increasingly familiar look on her face, a sort of world-weary expression which no mother wants for their child.

'I wish you would tell me what's troubling you, Sarah.'

Sarah shrugged off the question.

'Oh, it's nothing, Mummy. It's just this heat. It wears you down after a while, especially at night. I expect you have trouble sleeping, too.'

'It's not the heat that keeps me awake, darling.'

Sarah chose not to pursue her mother's somewhat cryptic remark. But it had brought back to mind what she had said a few nights previously, and it made her wonder — again — what exactly she had meant by it.

'The other night, Mummy, when you said goodnight to me, after the social for the opening day of the shoot . . . '

'Don't do anything your heart doesn't want to? Yes, I remember. Why?'

Sarah sighed.

'Well, it's not as simple as that, is it? I mean, if it was, and I chose to listen to my heart and not my head, people would be upset.'

Lady Patricia reached across and took Sarah's hand in hers.

'And is no-one you love upset at this

moment, my darling?'

Sarah could not meet Lady Patricia's gaze. The truth hurts.

'Of course there is, you know that.' Her manner was suddenly very defensive.

'My deepest wish has always been for your happiness, Sarah — your happiness, not your father's or that dreadful man, Fywell-Bennet — not even Robert Penfold if he makes you so unhappy.'

It was all too much. To hear Robert's name included broke her resolve to be strong. The tears poured down.

'Come here, my darling, come to your mother.'

Sarah sobbed loud and deeply into Lady Patricia's breast. All the misery and injustice came pouring out in uncontrollable outburst of spontaneous grief.

'There, there,' her mother whispered, stroking Sarah's hair in a tender and maternal fashion as the sobbing continued. Eventually, like the tide, it slowly started to ebb, until all that was coming from her was a succession of shuddering sighs.

After a few more minutes Sarah sat up, blew her nose and returned to her own chair, her mother all the time retaining a physical connection, with her hand in Sarah's. Both women grew silent for a little while, allowing what remained of any tension to evaporate.

Lady Patricia was the first to break the silence.

'Better?'

Sarah nodded, and blew her nose one more time.

'You know, I haven't always been so docile. When I was young — younger than you are now — I was a suffragette.'

Sarah's puffy eyes widened and her mouth gaped at this revelation.

'Yes, I know,' Lady Patricia said, noting her daughter's look of amazement. 'Hard to believe, isn't it? But I was. Not one of any great significance. By the time I joined the movement things were moving towards their goals.'

'Did you chain yourself to the railings ever?'

'No. Like I said, we were fast being recognised as a legitimate movement, so there were fewer violent demonstrations by the time I joined. Then, of course, the war came along and more or less put an end to any further activity.'

Sarah was looking at her mother in an altogether new light. It was so hard to believe or imagine that this, delicate, refined, unassuming person had once been a member of, what she knew of history, a violent, radical organisation.

Try as she might, Sarah could not place Lady Patricia in a situation where she would be a party to civil disobedience.

'You're shocked, I can see.'

'Well, yes. I mean, you just came out with it. How would you expect me to be?'

'I know. My own parents were horrified and lived in constant fear that I would be arrested and bring shame on the family.'

'Does Daddy know you were a suffragette?'

'Yes, he did. And what is more surprising, he supported me in that cause, even to the point of defending me against those — including his friends and his own family — who would claim we were all insane anarchists.

'There were many who would never speak to him again, friends he'd known from childhood. They all deserted him. But you see, he believed in me, he loved me for the person I was, and for no other reason.'

'But he seems so . . . conventional; so traditional.'

'Well, he is, and there's nothing wrong with that. He believes in this country, the Empire, the King. He believes in all these things. But there is in him, somewhere, that other person who also believes in the right of everyone to be true to themselves.'

Sarah frowned.

'Well, there's little sign of that now.'

Lady Patricia ignored the jibe.

'You know, you're not dissimilar to him yourself. You want the best of both worlds, but sometimes that's not always possible.'

'I would just like to be happy — and for everyone else to be — whichever world I'm in.'

'I know you do, dear, and in his own way so does your father. He's a complex man, Sarah, a contrary man, you might say.' She sighed, and looked across the garden at the few rose blooms still showing. 'You must remember that a lot of his plans and ambitions died with Michael, and he's finding it difficult to come to terms with that. And for some obscure reason he blames Robert for that — Robert survived and Michael didn't.'

Sarah was shocked.

'But that's awful, to wish someone else dead.'

Lady Patricia shook her head.

'No, dear, he didn't wish that, of course not. What he wished was that everything could be as it had been, before the war, which it patently isn't. Change, that's what is frightening him.'

Sarah nodded.

'I understand. It frightens me too, a little bit.'

'Exactly. And remember, he'd already fought through one war himself and had witnessed first-hand the dreadful cost to life and property and the inevitable changes that brought about. A second world war made things even less secure for people like us.'

The sun was making its slow progress towards the west as they spoke and Sarah, now facing its full glare, shifted her position to share her mother's shady spot.

'What you're saying, Mummy, is that Daddy will never accept Robert as anything other than his gamekeeper's son.'

'No, dear, what I'm saying is that I have been too cocooned in my own little world, enclosed in my own grief for Michael that I have neglected you and your own true feelings.'

Sarah sighed.

'But what's the point? I've heard that

Robert's got a job, so he'll be leaving soon. It's probably for the best. These chance meetings we have aren't doing either of us any good. What we both need is a fresh start.'

Lady Patricia looked keenly at her daughter.

'Does that mean you're going to take up the offer you've had?'

Sarah went scarlet.

'How did you know I'd had an offer?'

Lady Patricia smiled.

'I wasn't sure. I just put two and two together. Is it true then?'

'Would you like to see the letter?' Sarah was both excited and relieved at being able to share her good news.

'No, that's all right, just tell me about it.'

As Sarah did so, Lady Patricia did her best to conceal the shock that Sarah's news was causing her.

The Burning Question

With her memory of events leading to her collapse restored, Lady Patricia began to accumulate the results of her 'digging' with regard to Sir Percy Fywell-Bennet. And what had been unearthed was truly alarming.

Here was a man who had the temerity to assume that Sarah, daughter of a viscount and viscountess, would consider him as a suitable candidate for marriage.

The trusty butler, Foster, had proved more than useful on numerous occasions in making unpalatable discoveries surrounding Sir Percy and his 'habits,' the principal one being gambling, which had put him deeply into debt, to the point, Foster told her on good authority, that it could shortly make him bankrupt.

Lady Patricia was in a quandary as to what to do. Should she go to her husband and tell him of what she had learned, or should she confront Fywell-Bennet in order to shame him into giving up on the prospect of marrying Sarah?

Neither possibility filled her with any sort of confidence that the outcome would necessarily follow the course she would hope for. Her husband might not believe her and, through his blind stubbornness, might in fact speed up matters in order to get his own way.

As for Sir Percy, he was such a devious character that Lady Patricia could see him wriggling like a snake in order to extricate himself from her accusations. No, there was only one way of reaching the right resolution, and that was to consult the local oracle, Elizabeth Penfold. She rang for Foster.

'Yes, m'lady,' the old and loyal servant said, on entering the drawing-room.

'Foster, I have decided to seek advice as to what I should do with the information you have given me. Please ask Dodds to bring the car round, I shall be going out.'

★　★　★

Sarah's relief at confiding in her mother regarding her new employment was tempered by a nagging doubt that Lady Patricia was not altogether pleased with what she'd been told.

There was no one thing Sarah could put her finger on, just an impression of a lack of spontaneous enthusiasm on her mother's part.

She was mulling these things over as she walked from the Hall, across the gravelled sweeping drive, towards the stables.

She wasn't intending to go riding this morning. The heat was, if anything, more intense, and it wouldn't be fair to make Cymbeline leave the sheltered area of the paddock and suffer the heat just in order to please her.

No, a walk would better suit her anyway. It would give her thoughts a chance to spill out and put themselves into some sort of logical sequence.

But while she was in this introspective frame of mind, a harsh, loud abrasive noise broke into her thoughts in the shape of Sir Percy Fywell-Bennet's Aston Martin which now pulled up abruptly beside her, scattering small pieces of gravel, like shrapnel, all around.

Sarah had no need to look to guess who could be behind the wheel of the sports car, but her upbringing had taught her to always be polite, even to those whom you felt did not merit it.

'My dear Sarah, how nice to see you. And how delightful you look, too.' He openly ogled at Sarah in her summer frock, making her feel very uncomfortable.

'If you've come to see my father, he's not here, I'm afraid.' She offered no other explanation, and began to walk away, but Fywell-Bennet quickly leaped from his car and drew alongside her.

'Just a minute, my dear, what's the hurry?' He made to take hold of Sarah's elbow but she unceremoniously shook it off. 'I rather hoped you were going to be nice to me.'

Sarah turned to face him, fury written all. over her.

'Nice to you? The only reason I'm ever civil to you, Sir Percy, is out of deference to my parents, but that's as far as it goes. I've made myself perfectly clear that I want nothing to do with you.'

It was now Fywell-Bennet's turn to show his wrath.

'Now you listen to me, young lady. Whether you like it or not, you and I are going to become one, and I don't care how it's achieved. Unless of course,' he added, with that insufferable grin now spreading across his face, 'you want to see your boyfriend and his family evicted from their home.'

Sarah took a deep breath, trying to regain her composure.

'I have already agreed not to see Robert again, but that was not because I preferred your company to his. Now, if you will excuse me.' She turned and began walking away from him. 'I shall tell my father you called but I won't be able to tell him why.'

She set off on her walk at a much faster pace than she had originally intended, in an attempt to exorcise her anger.

The cheek of the man! His impertinence was beyond belief! But, gradually, as her realisation of his very real threats began to sink in, her pace slowed and her breathing settled into a steadier rhythm.

Without being conscious of going in any particular direction, her steps were taking her, almost instinctively upwards and onwards towards Westmoor wood, a familiar and much-loved place for all sorts of reasons.

Here, amongst the ancient oaks and beech trees, she found shade and quiet which had their effect on cooling her temper. She sat down under a particular beech tree — one that she had often shared with Robert and which offered a panoramic view of her home and estate — and tried not to think of anything else.

In a few minutes she was dozing off, only to be sharply woken by the shrill sounds of an excitable child.

'Come back here, you little beast!'

'Catch me if you can!'

The jumble of merry voices caused Sarah to sit up quickly and look round to see where they were coming from. She wasn't sure where, but she did know who those voices belonged to. It was Robert and Helen, his sister. The one was chasing the other through the wood, zig-zagging between the trees, laughing carelessly and causing the inhabitants of the wood to scatter vociferously in all directions as they did. Suddenly Helen stopped, just in time to prevent herself colliding into the now standing figure of Sarah.

'Miss Sarah,' the child said, breathlessly, as surprised to see her as Sarah was pleased to see both her and the rapidly approaching Robert.

'Hello, you two.' Sarah smiled, as now Robert drew up alongside his sister. 'You look as if you're having fun.'

'Fun?' Helen frowned. 'I should think not. Robert's threatened to tickle me to death if he catches me.'

Sarah smiled, looking from Robert — who also smiled — and then back again to the girl.

'Why would he want to do that, I wonder.'

'Because she's my little sister,' Robert said, with a grin. 'Isn't that reason enough?'

They all laughed, and then Helen spoke.

'Anyway, I must go. Mummy wants me to help her, er, do something or other . . . Bye.' And she ran off, her transparent excuse to leave her brother and Sarah alone together plainly clear to the two of them.

'I'll get you later,' Robert called after Helen's rapidly disappearing figure. Then he turned to Sarah. 'Why does she have to do everything at a hundred miles an hour?'

Sarah smiled.

'She's young, she's full of life and she wants to be everywhere at once. Surely you're not so old as to forget how you were very much the same when you were her age.' There was a hint of good-natured mockery that did not escape

Robert's notice.

'If I remember, you were pretty fast on your feet back then yourself.'

'Yes, and then Daddy bought me a pony so it could do the running for me from then on.'

Suddenly the spell was broken. The mention of Lord Trenton, and of his buying a pony for his daughter illustrated clearly how different and separate were their circumstances.

It had taken Robert years to save enough money, through odd jobs and accumulated birthday monies, to buy his first second-hand bike. No handouts for him. But then, of course, he wouldn't have expected any, any more than he would have expected Sarah to have to do a paper round in order to buy a pony. It was ridiculous.

At one time it hadn't occurred to him that Sarah was better than him, that he wasn't good enough for her. They were in love, and that was all that seemed to matter, which it did, initially.

It was really only because the

viscount had made his views known on the subject that he'd begun, himself, to have nagging doubts as to his worthiness to own Sarah's heart.

Yet, every time they happened to see each other again, for his part, his heart took over from his head and he was lost to common sense and reason once more.

'I'm glad I've seen you,' Sarah said. 'I wanted to clear something up.'

Robert was immediately on his guard, bracing himself for the worst.

'Go on,' he said, nervously.

'I wanted you to know that when you asked me to marry you . . .'

'It's all right, Sarah, you needn't say anything,' Robert interrupted, determined to spare her the embarrassment of explaining the pretty obvious reason why she would have, anyway, turned him down. He also wanted to spare himself the humiliation.

Sarah shook her head.

'Oh, but I do, Robert. You need to know. I may not have been certain what my answer would have been then — you did take me by surprise — but I do know what it would be now, that's if you'd still like to ask.'

Robert was puzzled. Sarah would hardly be so cruel as to make him go down on one knee again only to refuse him. But recent events had made him, if not suspicious, then cautious.

Things could hardly have changed to the extent that Lord Trenton would be viewing Robert as a future son-in-law, and these concerns were now holding him back from saying anything.

'Do you still love me, Robert?' She was looking at Robert with a sort of longing tempered by a fear that she was about to lose him forever by saying what she had.

Robert took a while to respond. He wanted so much to rush forward and take Sarah in his arms but he was afraid, too.

'I'll always love you, Sarah, always.'

'Then ask me.'

Still Robert hesitated. He imagined if

he went down on his knee again, the very action would conjure up that swine Fywell-Bennet. Sarah seemed to sense this.

'Just ask me Robert. Come here,' she beckoned, with outstretched arms.

But as he approached her, yet again a noise disturbed them. They both turned to look. What they could hear but yet not see was the sound or sounds of a horse's hooves coming ever closer. They both held their breath, clinging on to each other and staring towards where the sounds were coming from, getting ever closer.

Robert was first to react.

'Quick!' he whispered. 'Move back, into the wood. Come on!' He took her hand and led her deeper into the wood, stopping behind a wide-girthed oak tree from where they would be able to see, without being seen, what was the cause of their disturbance.

Dramatic Revenge

As Jack Penfold drove up the gravelled drive of Merefield Hall both he and Lord Trenton became aware of the car and its owner.

Sir Percy was still rooted to the spot where, minutes ago, Sarah had had the audacity to walk away from him. He watched the route she was taking, certain that it would lead up to Westmoor wood and an assignation with Robert Penfold. He was still pondering what to do about it when the gamekeeper's Land Rover pulled into the drive.

Lord Trenton, not best pleased to see Sir Percy, nevertheless greeted him courteously enough as he stepped from the vehicle.

'Ah, my dear Trenton.' Sir Percy was gushingly effusive in his greeting to the viscount.

'Sir Percy,' the viscount replied,

non-committally. 'What brings you here?'

They stood facing each other on the gravelled drive as Jack Penfold drove off.

'I fancied a ride, my lord, and knowing you had a sound stable I thought what could be better than to go for a hack on one of your steeds.'

Lord Trenton considered the request. On the whole it seemed a good idea to him. Get to know the fellow a bit better, he considered. Plus it was a glorious day for a ride. The almost savage heat of the sun had lessened, helped by a change in wind direction, giving the air a fresher feel.

'Very well. Have you brought anything suitable to wear?'

Sir Percy bounded round to the back of his car and opened up the boot. Amongst the riding apparel he had, surprisingly, had the foresight to bring with him a crop which he concealed within one of his boots.

'Is my car all right here?' the baronet

asked as they began to make their way across to the stable compound.

'It'll be fine. We're not expecting anyone.'

As they passed the paddock, Fywell-Bennet noticed Sarah's horse Cymbeline, and made a point of mentioning it to Lord Trenton.

'Do you think your daughter might wish to join us? I see her pony's in the paddock.'

Lord Trenton shook his head.

'Couldn't say. I don't know what she does or what she gets up to these days, and that's a fact.'

Sir Percy seized his opportunity.

'Perhaps she's still seeing that chappie, you know? Your gamekeeper's son.'

Again Lord Trenton shook his head.

'No, certainly not. She knows very well I wouldn't stand for it.'

'Good man, good man.' Sir Percy patted the viscount's back in rather a condescending fashion. 'Hopefully that means that . . . '

'Right, here we are. Choose your

mount.' Lord Trenton was glad of the opportunity to interrupt his guest. After all, nothing was yet decided. Sarah was not proving to be a very willing accomplice to his plan. And, as a matter of fact, Lord Trenton was beginning to understand why.

⋆ ⋆ ⋆

Lady Patricia had been watching all that had taken place, from the moment Sir Percy Fywell-Bennet arrived and confronted Sarah, to when her husband and the baronet had spoken, then set off towards the paddock.

She'd witnessed all these scenarios from the drawing-room, having been alerted by the loud engine noise of the Aston Martin and its subsequent braking, spreading gravel all across the neat drive.

She'd stood back from the casement window, partially concealed by a curtain. She could feel the anger rise in her throat as she watched Sarah's response to whatever Sir Percy had said to her, and felt proud and relieved to see her daughter marching away, head held high.

She was about to go outside and have words with the odious man when Lord Trenton, driven by Jack Penfold in the estate's land rover then turned up. Again she remained where she was, watching the conversation taking place between the two men as the Land Rover drove away.

She shuddered when Fywell-Bennet patted her husband on the back, as if he had done it to her. Then their figures walked out of her view in the direction of the stables.

She stepped out from the shadows, walking across to her armchair by the fire. But she did not sit down, she was in a too agitated state to do that. Instead, she picked up her bag from the occasional table, rifling through it till she found what she was searching for. Now she would wait.

★ ★ ★

Convinced that he would discover Sarah and Robert together, Sir Percy urged his horse onwards and upwards, much to Lord Trenton's disapproval.

'Hoy, Bennet, ease up! Ease up, I say!' But, impelled, by his mission, Sir Percy continued to dig his heels hard into his mount's flanks. He was convinced he would find Sarah and Robert together at the top — together and without a rational explanation as to why they should both be there.

This, he felt, would surely fire up Lord Trenton to take immediate and irreversible action against the whole Penfold family, placing Sarah in a position of unconditional surrender, especially when Sir Percy would show his compassionate side and beg the viscount to spare all but the son, Robert.

As long as he could be removed from the scene the baronet felt, through some sort of misplaced vanity, that he would be free to win over Sarah's affections.

However, as he reached the top of the incline at the edge of the wood phase one of his plans were already in disarray. There was no sign of the couple, and he didn't dare explore deeper into the wood due to its many low, overhanging branches and uneven pathways.

His temper was almost at boiling point as Lord Trenton finally reached the summit and drew alongside him, looking and feeling just as angry himself.

'For heaven's sake, man, what are you thinking of? Look at your horse, look at the sweat on it.'

Sir Percy did not look at the sweat on his horse. Instead he looked at the face of Lord Trenton, sneering as he did.

'Your daughter was up here with that peasant of a boyfriend of hers.'

Lord Trenton looked around him.

'Where? When?'

'Oh, I'm sure they've gone now — gone to find some other love nest . . . '

Lord Trenton almost went purple with rage.

'How dare you speak about my daughter in such a way, you have absolutely no right to do so. Take it back!' As he said these words he was aware that he was speaking in passionate defence of his daughter — but also of Robert.

The gamekeeper's son might not be a gentleman by the standards known to the aristocracy, but he was a good man, an honourable man, who would never treat his daughter with anything less than respect.

The sneer deepened on Fywell-Bennet's face, making him look even more repulsive than usual.

'You're an old fool, Trenton.' He spat out the words with all the contempt that had been bottling up inside him for months now. He turned his horse to take him back down the slope and, as he did, he pulled from his sleeve the riding crop which he'd concealed till now. Lord Trenton, with his back to Sir Percy, did not see the baronet strike the viscount's horse with all the force he could muster.

The immediate result of this was for the whipped horse to scream in pain and rear up. Lord Trenton tried to calm the poor creature but the whites of its eyes were giving every indication of fear and panic which then manifested itself in the form of a frantic gallop into the wood.

Sarah and Robert had been listening to all that had gone on, but now they became seriously alarmed at hearing, first of all, the pained and distressed cries of Lord Trenton's mount, and then the even more disturbing sound of thundering hooves getting ever closer, coupled with the desperate calls for the creature to stop.

Ever closer the sounds came, and with those sounds the crashing and snapping of branches and undergrowth. Suddenly Robert stepped out from the cover of the tree.

Like a train tearing down the tracks, the horse and its rider were heading straight for him. But the rider was not sitting upright, he was slumped on to the horse's shoulder.

Robert stood in the creature's path, legs apart, and, stretching out his arms, waited for what would happen. Sarah had also left her hiding place but was stopped now as she saw what Robert was attempting to do.

At first it appeared that the frightened animal, in its blind panic, was not aware of Robert's presence, but as it got nearer — and without losing speed — it started to change direction. But Robert had placed himself firmly in a spot where there was no way round or past him. The horse, with nowhere else to go, reared up just a few feet in front of the immoveable Robert, whinnying loudly as it did.

Sarah saw her opportunity and rushed forward, grabbing Perseus's bridle as the horse's front legs returned to earth. At the same time Robert ran past her to catch the limp, falling figure of Lord Trenton, laying him a little distance away on the ground. The viscount, though dazed, was conscious. He had a cut on his forehead where he'd struck a branch as the horse bolted into the unfamiliar darkness of the wood.

'Is he all right?' he whispered. 'Is Perseus all right?'

Robert, now understanding what Lord Trenton was talking about, smiled.

'He's fine, sir. Sarah's got hold of him.'

'Sarah? Sarah's here?'

'Yes, my lord. Now, if you'll just let me sit you up and lean you against this tree I'll carry out a bit of first aid.'

Having got the viscount in position, Robert set about seeing to his wound. Taking off his own shirt, Robert then tore the whole of one sleeve from it and wrapped it around the viscount's head, covering and stemming the flow of his injury.

'Is he all right, Robert?' Sarah's voice carried a note of alarm in it which Perseus sensed, making the horse agitated. Sarah had to turn her attention back to the animal and reassure it all was well.

Robert nodded. Satisfied that the bandage he'd made was holding good, he turned to Sarah.

'Do you think you could take Perseus

back to the stables and then phone for Doctor Anderson? Tell him we'll need a stretcher to get your father back down. I'll stay here with him till you get back.'

Sarah nodded, then turned Perseus, who was totally passive now, back towards the entrance to the woods. Robert watched until they were both out of sight.

Lord Trenton, who had been watching Robert with a keen eye, despite his injuries, put out a hand, touching Robert's arm to gain his attention.

'Are you all right, sir? The doctor will be here soon. Are you cold?'

Lord Trenton smiled.

'You love Sarah, don't you?'

Robert breathed in deeply, unsure of what his reply might cause. Still, it was the truth and he would not deny it, even to the man most opposed to their relationship.

'I do, sir, very much. I always have, if you must know.'

★　★　★

Lady Patricia was standing by Sir Percy's car, waiting for his return. She'd seen him part of the way down the slope, riding back from the woods, although there was no sign of her husband.

This did not necessarily worry her, as she knew Lord Trenton had never been very keen to spend more time than was absolutely necessary in that insufferable man's company.

She watched him until he went out of sight, heading back to the stables. She remained where she was.

At first she heard his approach, the rapid footsteps crunching the gravel. Then, as he came round into view, he then noticed her.

'Ah, Sir Percy, there you are. I trust you had a good ride.'

'What do you want?' All trace of contrived courtesy were gone now. He just wanted to be away from this place and this infernal family.

Lady Patricia was not to be intimidated and stood her ground.

'I have something for you.'

Despite his ill temper, there was a flicker of interest that changed — very slightly — the look on his disagreeable face. He now stood by the door of his car facing Lady Patricia.

'Well?'

'First of all I want to share with you some of those things you have tried to keep secret from us.'

Sir Percy scowled.

'What on earth are you talking about?' He glanced back nervously towards the track he'd just descended. Lady Patricia noticed and looked, herself, in that direction.

'Are you looking for someone? My husband, perhaps?'

A sudden change came over Sir Percy. He looked fearful, as if Lord Trenton's wife knew what had happened. But of course she couldn't have. She would have been a lot less calm if she had known.

'You said you had something for me,' he said, trying to distract her from what she'd previously said.

She went on to name as many of the

people and institutions that Foster had managed to discover who were owed money — in some cases very large sums of money. She also drew his attention to his war record, which wasn't quite as distinguished as he would have everyone believe.

'Does the name Lilian Parkin mean anything to you?' she asked finally. 'Oh yes, I can see by the look on your face that it does. She's the 'lady' you have been involved with, to put it politely, while all the time you have been attempting to coerce my husband into agreeing to allow my daughter to accept your hand in marriage.'

Sir Percy, red-faced and furious, said nothing but got into his car. He would have driven off immediately but could not find his car key.

'Is this what you're looking for, Sir Percy?' Lady Patricia dangled the key before him, just out of reach. 'You should be more careful where you leave it.' She tossed the key at him but he failed to catch it and had to scramble about in the restricted space of the footwell to retrieve it.

'One final thing, Sir Percy. As I said, I have something for you.' She took from her clasp bag the folded piece of paper that she had been looking for earlier. 'I'd like you to have this. I think you have enough on your plate without the worry of paying me back.'

Starting up the engine, he snatched the IOU from Lady Patricia's hand and drove off at a reckless speed, scattering gravel.

Lady Patricia watched him go, feeling an immense sense of relief. As she stood there, the realisation of the significance of what Elizabeth Penfold had told her now hit her with startling clarity.

'He'll bring himself down on another man's mount,' she had said, but it made no sense — at the time — to Lady Patricia. 'But you will hold the horse power.' Again, nothing at the time. She had been beginning to think that this had been a wasted journey, but something made her sit it through.

Elizabeth Penfold had looked up from her cards.

'You'll pay him back,' she told the viscountess, 'and he won't dare refuse. You hold the key.'

Thinking of it now, it was like the unravelling of a riddle. She might have dwelt on it a little longer but, as she turned back to the Hall, she noticed people hurriedly making their way up the slope to Westmoor wood. One looked not unlike Doctor Anderson. Another appeared to be carrying a stretcher.

New Beginnings

The church was full. Everyone from everywhere seemed to be there, plus those outside, waiting for a glimpse of the bride and groom.

It was the first wedding to be held in the new building and, although Lord Trenton might have preferred it to have taken place either at his chapel or at least in the village, he had accepted Sarah's wishes in the matter.

They'd had to get a special licence for the occasion, as it was technically outside of Sarah's parish, but that had been overcome with a word or two in the right place by the viscount.

After all, the land the new church stood on had been his land before the compulsory purchase, so it could be argued that it was still in the parish of St Edmunds, the village church.

By way of appeasing any misgivings

on the part of Lord Trenton, both Sarah and Robert had agreed for a blessing of their marriage to take place, later, at the family chapel. But for the wedding itself it had become almost a matter of principle.

They wanted it to be seen as an indication of where their future life lay — not in the past but in the future, where man and wife would co-exist on an equal footing.

Again, Lord Trenton had his doubts, but Sarah's earnestness and Lady Patricia's persuasion had finally convinced him that this was the way forward for them all.

After all, he had seen for himself how deeply in love and committed to each other they were, and Robert's bravery, quick thinking and selflessness had saved the viscount from serious harm.

For bridesmaids, Sarah had her best friend Mandy and Robert's sister Helen. It was strange to see Helen so dressed up, not in her usual tomboy outfit, and she looked so pretty that even she was pleased with her appearance.

Robert had chosen his father to be best man, and he'd risen to the occasion with quiet pride.

'I'm sorry that I've caused you so much worry over Sarah and me,' he'd said to Jack Penfold when he brought up the subject of best man, 'but I'm hoping that's all in the past now.'

His father stood up and, much to Robert's surprise, shook his son's hand vigorously.

'I'd be glad to,' he said, almost — but not quite — smiling.

Jack had heard first hand from Lord Trenton himself about what had happened in the woods and had been assured that the viscount would be proud to have Robert as his son-in-law.

'Times are changing,' Lord Trenton told the astonished gamekeeper, 'and it's going to be a change for the better.'

★ ★ ★

The morning of the wedding, a Saturday, was warm and sunny, a bonus for mid-September, and shafts of light beamed through the tall stained-glass windows of the modern church as Sarah and Robert exchanged vows.

Seated behind them, in the front seats — not pews here — both Sarah's parents looked on, each with an immense feeling of pride and affection for both young people.

'They're a lovely couple,' Lady Patricia whispered in her husband's ear.

'They are indeed, my dear,' he agreed as he took her hand in his. All trace of any injury he'd suffered as a result of Fywell-Bennet's assault had gone now.

The stretcher had proved to be just a precaution. Dr Anderson had recommended aspirin and complete rest for a day or so, which gave Lord Trenton time to reflect on what had happened and what he'd seen.

It reminded him of how he had felt for his wife when they had first fallen in love all those years ago. They had faced similar prejudices and had managed to overcome them.

But he'd never been tested in the way that Robert had been; had not had to show such courage as Robert did in order to save the life of a man he would have been perfectly entitled to think of as an enemy. But it was over now.

Robert may not have had a title to his name but he was a far better man than Sir Percy Fywell-Bennet could ever hope to be.

★ ★ ★

With the service over, everyone began making their way to the old barn where the reception was to take place.

Sarah and Robert travelled in one of the estate's wagons, suitably decorated with flowers and bunting. They smiled and waved at all the confetti-throwing well-wishers as the old carthorse made its plodding way towards the old barn.

'Well, Mrs Penfold, how does it feel to be a respectable married woman?'

Sarah grinned.

'Wonderful, absolutely wonderful.

How about you?'

'This has been the happiest day of my life.' He leaned forward and kissed Sarah on the lips, her response as passionate as his.

'I'm sorry we can only get away for the weekend, but until the holidays we can't do better.'

'We're both in the same boat, remember? Me being your school's secretary.'

It had only come to light that both Sarah and Robert would be working at the new school when they encountered each other on their first day there.

'Still, I don't mind,' she continued. 'It's being together that matters; no more keeping it secret. Oh, I do love you so much, Robert,' she added, spontaneously wrapping her arms around her husband.

'Anyway,' Robert said, as they finally drew apart, 'it will give us a chance to settle into our new home, our brand new home.'

'Oh, yes,' Sarah agreed excitedly. She took on a wistful expression. 'Forty-eight Laxton Avenue. I like how they've named all the roads after all the different types of fruit Daddy used to grow there.'

Robert frowned.

'Are you sure you don't mind? After all, it's a lot to give up.'

'No, I don't. Do you, then?'

'Not at all. After all, an Englishman's home is his castle.'

And they embraced again as the old carthorse continued its steady progress towards the old barn where, barely a year before, it had hosted the harvest supper.

We do hope that you have enjoyed reading this large print book.

Did you know that all of our titles are available for purchase?

We publish a wide range of high quality large print books including:
Romances, Mysteries, Classics
General Fiction
Non Fiction and Westerns

Special interest titles available in large print are:
The Little Oxford Dictionary
Music Book, Song Book
Hymn Book, Service Book

Also available from us courtesy of Oxford University Press:
Young Readers' Dictionary
(large print edition)
Young Readers' Thesaurus
(large print edition)

For further information or a free brochure, please contact us at:
Ulverscroft Large Print Books Ltd.,
The Green, Bradgate Road, Anstey,
Leicester, LE7 7FU, England.
Tel: (00 44) **0116 236 4325**
Fax: (00 44) **0116 234 0205**

DUKE IN DANGER

Fenella J. Miller

Lady Helena Faulkner agrees to marry only if her indulgent parents can find a gentleman who fits her exacting requirements. Wild and unconventional, she has no desire for romance, but wants a friend who will let her live as she pleases. Lord Christopher Drake, known to Helena as Kit, her brother's best friend, needs a rich wife to support his mother and siblings. It could be the perfect arrangement. But when malign forces do their best to separate them, can Helena and Kit overcome the disasters and find true happiness?